Threads of Blue

To Delilah

Abby Kramer

Threads of Blue

The following is a work of fiction. Any names, character, places, and events are the product of the author's imagination. Any resemblence to persons, living or dead, is entirely coincidental.

ISBN: 978-0-9979902-0-1

Editor
Daniel Johnson

Cover Art
Photagrapher: Haley Stone
Model: Emily Gassaway
Designer: Abigail R. Cramer

Acknowledgements

While constructing this novella, a lot of people have guided and encouraged me throughout the process of publishing. I would sincerely like to thank the following people.

Ashly Brophy, Kim Davidson, Emily Gassaway, Rhonda Henderson, Daniel Johnson, Nicole Roseveare, Haley Stone, Amy Warren, Matt Warren, my mom and dad, my best friends Lynsie and Adrian, and my peers from Nicole's fiction writing class.

For Tyler

Threads of Blue

By: Abigail R. Cramer

Chapter 1

"Did you remember to put extra socks in your suitcase?" Mom asked, heaving a bag into the back of our old van.

"Yeah, Mom," I grumbled.

I started to walk back toward the house when Mom said, "Oh!" as if she'd just remembered something important. "Andrea, did you check the mail? Maybe you got something about your scholarship for Denver."

My mood darkened at the thought. "No," I said. "I mean, I checked, but I didn't get anything...but mom?" I thought of the envelope that was now stuffed into the front pocket of my suitcase. It had arrived in April. I wasn't sure why I brought it, maybe to keep my dad from finding it.

"Yeah?" she said, mostly focused on

getting everything to fit just right.

I took a deep breath. "I was thinking that maybe I don't wanna do soccer next year. I kinda just—"

She whipped her head around. "What? No, no, no. We spent *way* too much time preparing that application."

"Well, can I at least stay home so I'm here when it comes?" I said with a smirk.

She sighed. "Andy, I don't know why you're so reluctant to go on this trip. It'll be fun. I promise." She gave me a reassuring smile.

I was almost eighteen. My mom didn't listen to a word I said, although I didn't listen to her much either.

"I don't even like camping," I said as I handed her my suitcase. "*You* don't even like camping."

She gave me a look that meant that the discussion was over. "Go get your brother and make sure he doesn't forget his inhaler."

This was going to be a *brilliant* start to my summer.

"Tony!" I yelled, stomping up the stairs. No response. "Tony!" I yelled louder, standing outside his room. Still nothing. "I'm coming in!" I announced and threw the door open.

Tony yelped, looking up from a copy of Hustler magazine. I tried not to imagine what he'd been doing.

A big old pair of over-ear headphones

sat on his head."Yeah?" he finally answered, trying to sound casual while pulling half of the headset off so it revealed one of his ears.

My brother had our father's facial features, which meant he was decent looking, in the face anyway. His body, however, did not reflect any relation to my father; he was scrawny and well into that awkward stage of puberty, with little wispy hairs starting to pop up on his upper lip. He had yet to attempt shaving, and was probably unaware of the necessary grooming that would come with impending manhood.

"Really? You know normal people use the internet?" I said, giving him a disapproving look. "And you're gonna go deaf with how loud you play that music."

He rolled his eyes at me, but was still blushing a little. "What do you want?"

"It's time to go," I said shifting my weight, "and mom said don't forget your inhaler."

He hopped up from his bed. "But Dad's not home."

That was fine with me. "You can call him later if you really want to. He should have been here on time."

He made a face like he'd just tasted something sour.

"Just hurry up," I told him, "Mom's waiting."

During the drive, the rain seemed

to create a curtain over everything we passed. Tony had his headphones on, ignoring the outside world. Meanwhile, my mom was tapping her fingers on the steering wheel to the Fish radio station. The road stretched out in front of us, with rolling grassy hills on both sides. Out ahead I saw little booths. A road sign read: Welcome to California. I deduced that the booths must have been those checkpoints where they ask if you have produce. Four hours had passed since we'd arrived there.

"Mom..." I said, "where are we going? We've never gone out of state for a camping trip before."

My mom looked at me for second, smiled, and turned her face back to the road. "A friend recommended a new site for us to visit. It's just a little farther."

"Oh..." I said, still feeling unsure. I hated surprises.

Tony, probably noticing the booths in the distance, took off his headphones. "Mom?"

"Yeah honey?"

"Can I use your phone? I need to call Dad." Mom was really against the idea of us kids having cell phones for some reason. Tony stared into the rear view mirror waiting for a response.

She glanced to the dashboard where the phone sat and bit her bottom lip. "My phone's almost dead. We'll stop after we cross into California and you can use a payphone."

"Okay," my brother said, looking at me as if to ask what I thought. I shrugged.

After passing through the checkpoint, my mom pulled over at a rest stop just a couple miles down. It was good to get out of the car and stretch. It had finally stopped raining. After we'd finished in the restroom, my mom and I got back in the car and waited for Tony. Moments later, he came up to the car and tapped on the driver's side window. My mom rolled the window down.

"Mom, I need some quarters," he said.

"Okay." She dug around in her purse for a moment. "Actually, I don't think I have any right now." She smiled apologetically at Tony and he started to head for the back seat.

"Wait a second. You barely even looked." I grabbed the purse from my mom's lap.

"Andy!" she scolded, tugging it away from my hands with surprising force. She looked at me and her face softened a bit. "That was rude. Please don't ever take something of mine without permission."

My brother and I barely spoke for the remainder of the drive. My mother, however, didn't stop talking. Maybe she was trying to ease the tension, but she was simply drawing attention to it.

"Have I ever told you two about my cousin Darla?" she asked with an awkward smile.

Tony wasn't paying much attention and I just replied with a simple, "No," because all I could think about was how strange my mother was behaving. She was not one of those moms who was friends with their kids. She tended not to make any conversation that was overly personal.

"Well," she started gleefully, as if telling me about a TV show she'd recently watched, "I grew up in Tennessee with your grandpa and my grandmother, but you already know that. When I was in my teens...I was say...hmm...maybe I was twelve. Anyway, my uncle moved in next door. He and his wife just had their fourth child, which was my cousin Darla, and let me tell you, she was a fussy baby. You and Tony were so easy compared to her. They already had three kids and they were really hard working people (my uncle was the pastor at our church, really good man) so I helped them take care of the kids sometimes."

I always thought my mom belonged with country folk.

While my mother rambled on, it dawned on me that this was not only the first time she'd mentioned Darla, but it was the first time she'd mentioned being a kid. It seemed that the only part of her life she'd ever talked about was with our dad. My dad told us all sorts of stories about being in boy scouts, being on the football team, and things like that, but as far as I could recall, my mom had never mentioned her childhood.

It got late, really late. Around midnight, I asked my mom where we were going, because we obviously weren't going camping. She acted like she didn't hear me.

"Mom," I repeated, "Where are we going?"

She hunched over her steering wheel, like an animal protecting its young from a predator. Tony was asleep in the backseat.

I shoved at her shoulder. "Mom!"

"Andy! Don't do that while I'm driving!" she bellowed as if she feared for her life. The car hadn't even swerved.

I gave her my best stink eye. "Where are we going?"

"Just shut up already," she growled and reached for her purse. I was aghast, my mouth agape. She'd never told me to shut up before. She dug in her purse with one hand while keeping her eyes on the road, pulling out bits of paper and glancing down quickly to see what they were. She tossed away napkins, coupons, and receipts until she finally found what she was looking for. She shook out a folded up piece of paper and shoved it at me. On it were directions to an address in…"Reno, Nevada?" I raised an eyebrow at her. "You're kidding, right?"

"Read me the directions when we get to Reno," she demanded, yet again ignoring my question. I guess she wasn't kidding. A pit had begun to form in my stomach. Where was she taking us?

I did as she asked, and in the early morning we arrived at a little flat-roofed house in Reno. My mom got out of the van, slammed the door shut behind her and headed for the front door.

"Where are we?" asked Tony, wiping the sleep from his eyes.

I shook my head, staring intensely at my mother as she knocked on the screen. A small woman with dark hair stepped out.

"Come on," I instructed, getting out of the car.

Tony followed obediently.

My mother gave us a full pearled smile. "This," she said with a shimmer of sweat on her brow, "is my cousin Darla."

I had seen my mother be two-faced on many occasions. I'd seen her get in an argument with my father and answer the phone as if nothing was amiss, and how she could talk sweetly to someone she hated; so I knew that smile well. Darla matched that smile. I knew something was wrong. Something was really wrong.

Darla put a hand on my shoulder. "It's nice to meet you, Andy."

I took a step back to free myself from her touch. She addressed my brother unfazed. "You too, Tony."

Despite the introductions, the tone of her voice made it sound as if she already knew us. I tried once again to get answers. "Why are we here?"

Darla whipped her head around. "You haven't told them?" She exchanged a knowing glare with my mom. "Oh boy," she muttered.

At first, I was confused, but suddenly old memories came flooding in. There was that guilty look on my dad's face and the naked woman on the desk in his study.

"You're gonna stay here a while until your mom finds a place for you all."

I felt sick. I leaned over, trying to stifle the peanut butter and jelly from dinner that was working its way back up my system.

"What?" Tony yelled, paying no attention to me. "So you're just moving us away from dad? Did you even tell him? What the fuck, Mom?"

"This is crazy." Despite everything I knew, I couldn't help despising my mother in that moment. "How can you just decide to move us away without asking us first? We have lives, you know, and friends!" I instantly thought of my best friends, Nicole and Justin.

"Nice shirt," Justin teased. "It would be better if it was wet."

I expressed what I thought of his comment by way of a non-verbal hand gesture.

"What's up your butt today?" he snorted as he sat down across from me at the lunch table.

Nicole rolled her eyes at him. "She's having a bad day. Mr. Cappal is not gonna give her an A in his class."

"Oh. Mr. Cappal's up your butt?" he said, laughing at his own joke.

"You don't get it," I explained. "I promised my parents I'd get all As this semester and he told me that if I don't get a 98 or higher on my essay, I won't get an A in the class. Why do we have to write about ancient Chinese poetry anyway? It doesn't mean anything. It's just descriptions of trees."

Nicole crossed her arms. "Well, if you didn't want to write bullshit papers, you shouldn't have taken AP World Literature. I hate to be that person, but you kind of set yourself up."

I shot Nicole an evil look.

"Anyway…" she continued, "you shouldn't worry about having perfect grades or whatever. Why don't you focus on figuring what you're gonna major in. I mean, we're like only four months away from graduating and you don't even have a plan."

"Oh yeah?" I said, my rage stewing. "What's your plan?"

"Well, I'm going to nursing school. Heck, even Justin has a plan. Right, Justin?" He nodded and mumbled something through a mouth full of food.

She sniffled. "As your mom, I have to make hard decisions. I—"

I cut her off. "That's bullshit! You didn't do this for us. You're selfish."

My mom looked as if she were injured. "Andy…"

I turned away. I couldn't stand to look at her. Both of my parents were pathetic; my dad with his affair and my mom with her delusions of us living in Nevada, the desert of all places. My mother was certifiable.

"Go get your bags," Darla said, trying to ease the tension. "We'll talk about this when everyone's found their heads." Darla was shorter than my mom, and obviously younger. She had high cheekbones and styled her hair in tight curls that almost seemed to be a helmet around her head. She spoke in a high register and had a slight southern accent. She looked at Tony and me and smiled. "Why don't you two get some sleep. I'd like to catch up with your momma. Then later today, you guys can go out and have some fun." Her suggestion sounded just fine to me. I was exhausted and ready for bed. She showed us to the guest room, which had two twin beds, and said that she'd see us in a few hours.

Our room was decorated with old floral wallpaper, and there were two lamps hanging from the wall beside each of our headboards wearing faded pink lamp shades that omitted a yellow glow. The whole room reminded me of a crusty motel. I flopped down onto my bed. Tony was changing into his pajama pants. He took his inhaler out of his jean pocket and placed it on the night stand.

"Goodnight," Tony said, turning off the light next to his bed.

I did the same with mine and flipped over on my side. "Goodnight."

Chapter 2

When I woke up, my brother was already gone. According to the clock on the nightstand between our beds it was two in the afternoon. I couldn't believe I'd slept so late. I immediately got ready for the day. I showered and studied my face in the bathroom mirror. My eyes looked darker than normal and I could have sworn I was growing frown lines. I had a very slender face and thick eye-brows. My hair was a caramel color and fell perfectly straight no matter what I did to it; I only recently decided to hack it all off, well most of it, it was about jaw length. I looked just like my mom, unfortunately, but the same brown eyes as my dad. I got dressed in my shorts and army green tank and headed out. My mom and Darla were sitting in the kitch-en. "Where's Tony?" I asked, rubbing my eyes. My mom met my eyes, taking a sip of her coffee.

"He already left. I think he went to the park," Darla said. "You can go meet him, it's just down the street."

A few minutes later, I was standing in the park, scanning my surroundings, which included things you would commonly see at a local park. There were trimmed patches of grass for children to play on, white daisies, worn out swings and a twisty plastic slide. But one of these things did not belong, and it was my brother, who, much to my shock, was nonchalantly smoking what looked like a joint from where I was standing. Unaware I had spotted him, he stood next to the park bathrooms, the building casting a shadow over him. "Tony!" I yelled, jogging over to him. "You have asthma!" I snatched the joint away from him. "Where did you even ge—"

Until that moment, I hadn't noticed the girl who was standing less than a foot away from Tony. She had blue hair and great big eyes to match. Her black lace skirt, tattered leggings, and the plastic rainbow beads that covered both her arms told me she was someone trying desperately to stand out from the crowd, but who, ironically, perfectly fit the build of another stereotype: the "emo kid," a self-described outcast who wanted to be seen.

"I'm sorry," the girl apologized. "I didn't know."

"It's okay," I said.

I don't know why I said that; it was clearly not okay.

She smiled. "Want a hit?"

I let out a big sigh. "Sure, why not? I might as well."

"Andy?" Tony's jaw dropped down to his chest. He shook his head in disbelief. "I'm going back to Darla's."

As Tony walked away from us, the girl's grin grew wider. "I'm Max. I'm guessing you're Andy."

"Yep." I kicked a pebble off the walkway.

"So, what's up?"

"I'm just visiting, I guess. We're staying with my mom's cousin Darla," I said in one breath.

She threw her head back in a cackle. "Oh, yeah! The lady with all the kids."

"I didn't know she had kids."

"Sure does," Max said, twirling away from the bathrooms, joint in hand. "She's got like five of 'em."

"Oh wow."

"They must be at their dad's." She took another puff and moved a little closer to me. "I like your cut. Very edgy," she said while inhaling.

I ran my fingers through my hair. The stylist had called it a wedge and it was the shortest I'd had it since the first grade. I felt my face getting hot and hoped I wasn't blushing. "Thanks. I just cut it."

She took another step toward me. We were nose to nose and without much warning, she kissed me.

Despite what you'd think someone's lips might taste like after they'd just been smoking pot, there was a touch of sweetness, like cherries or perhaps strawberry? For a moment, my mind was focused on trying to figure out the flavor of her lip balm, until the gravity of the situation set in. I was kissing a girl. My head felt heavy. *Why would she kiss me?* I suddenly felt exposed and self-conscious, like I was being watched. I pulled away.

"Nice to meet you," she exclaimed as if we'd just shaken hands.

"I gotta go," I said looking away.

"No. Don't go," Max protested with puppy dog eyes.

I started to respond, but she stopped me. "I'm going to see my friend Daenan. Wanna go? He lives real close."

I hesitated, unable to get the sensation of the kiss out of my system, "I don't know..."

"It'll be fun," she pleaded.

"Okay. Sure," I said finally.

The apartments where Daenan lived were just two blocks from the park. The buildings were in serious need of a paint job and just coming into the complex, I was overwhelmed with the stench of cigarettes. The pavement beneath us was cracked and uneven. Max led me to apartment 11A. She pounded on the door. I heard what could only be described as "screamo music" coming through the door. The shrill, eardrum-piercing vocals and crunch of heavy power cords were unmistakable to that uncouth subgenre. "Daenan!" she hollered. "Open up!"

"Maxine!" A woman's voice called down from the upper floor. "Get that boy to turn down that racket!"

"Okay," Max answered. "Sorry, miss Johnson!"

She pounded on the door again. This time it opened.

"Hey slut," he greeted. He was well built, with olive skin, and I could see a small tattoo peeking out from his t-shirt colar.

"Hey!" she shoved at him playfully and led me inside.

"Who's this?" Daenan nodded his head at me.

"This is—"

"I'm Andy."

He smirked, gave a little, "Hmp," and went into the living room to turn down the music. Then he plopped down on the couch and picked up a Playstation controller that was sitting on the coffee table. Max let herself flop over the arm of the couch so that she landed on her back with her head resting on Daenan's lap. She reached up and stroked his jaw. He showed little interest, clearly immersed in a game of Grand Theft Auto instead.

"Come on..." she whined, "play with us."

He raised a brow, not taking his eyes off the screen. "What do you mean, 'play'?"

Frankly, I was wondering the same thing.

Max expended an over-dramatic sigh. "I don't know...we could get some Fireball, call some people, and head over to the graveyard."

He frowned. "Eh, not tonight. I'd rather stay in and *play* here." He turned his head away from the screen a second and gave another smirk like the one he had given me when I'd first arrived. "Does your friend like to *play*?" He licked his lips.

I stared at him. "No thanks."

Max laughed, swatting at his chest. "Daenan, don't be gross."

"I'm not being gross," he scowled, "I'm being friendly."

"Well, she doesn't want to play," her voice dropped to a slightly more serious tone. "Andy's innocent."

"Uh," I said, feeling a little defensive, "I beg to differ."

He ignored me. "Like what," he said to Max, "compared to you?" He threw his head back, laughing like it was the funniest thing ever said.

"Screw you," she said baring her teeth and sat up so she was also facing the TV. "Why are you being such a dick today?"

"I'm sorry," Daenan said. "Why don't you just run home to daddy?" he snarled.

Max stomped her foot and propelled herself from the couch. "Fuck you."

"Let's just go," I said.

Max lived in the same complex as Daenan. Outside of Max's apartment was a broken planter with the soil spilling out of the side and a garbage bag that appeared to be filled with empty beer bottles that hung on a nail to the left of the welcome mat. Max noticed I was looking and blushed. "My dad had some friends over last night."

"Oh." I paused for a moment. "Max, it's okay."

She smiled. "You're sweet. I don't think he's home if you wanna come in."

I could feel my face getting hot. My mind flashed back to our kiss, the way it felt. I knew that if I went inside, there would be expectations, or at the very least, I'd have to fight off unwanted advances. She was pretty, I suppose, but I was not interested in hooking up with a girl. I didn't like girls. They were too... doesn't matter. I just wasn't going to do it. "I'm going to head home. See you later."

"Okay," she said, and slowly shut the door.

I stared at my ceiling for probably three hours that night. Was I a lesbian? There was no way. I couldn't be.

"What took you so long at the park today?" Tony asked, startling me. Up until then I had thought he was asleep.

"We were just talking." This was the first time I'd ever directly lied to my brother. "Why did you smoke pot with a random stranger anyway?"

"Well I..." he muttered, "I guess I just... never mind. It's stupid."

"Just say it."

He sighed. "I guess I just thought she was pretty, I guess."

My face felt hot again.

At that moment, we heard a tap at our window. I looked over and saw Max. I glanced at the clock that sat on the nightstand between our beds; it was already after four. I looked at Tony, who looked as surprised as I was. She gestured for me to open the window. I did.

"What are you doing here?" I felt like I was shouting, even though I was only speaking in a whisper.

"I had to get out of the house," she said as if that answered the question and pulled herself into the window.

When the light hit her face, her eyelid and a large surrounding portion of her face shimmered a rotten purple.

"Holy shit!" Tony exclaimed. "What happened?"

Max laughed. "My dad's a drunk."

Tony and I exchanged concerned looks.

"It's okay," she tried to reassure us. "Can I just stay here tonight?"

I hesitated for a moment, but Tony spoke up before I could think of an answer. "Yeah," he said, "I'll get you a blanket."

We laid down for bed, with Max on the floor, and we didn't really speak. Tony and I turned out the lights beside our beds, and in the dark a somber heaviness fell on the room. Seeing someone after they've been hit is a shock to say the least, let alone having a girl you just met climb into your new bedroom window with a fresh shiner. I wasn't sure how to feel about it, and in the suffocating quiet, I couldn't sleep. Then after a while I heard a soft whimpering buried beneath the silence.

I tried to ignore it. I needed sleep, and I didn't want to bring up anything unpleasant in fear that we'd all be forced to stay up even longer going through the whole story. But as I lay there, I began to grow nauseous, which made it even harder to sleep. The crying was getting to me and I had to say something.

I sat up and turned on the light. "Max," I said, "are you okay?"

She sat with her legs tucked under her and chuckled mirthlessly. "I'm fine."

She wiped her tears away, smudging thick black tar across her cheeks. Her eyes were red and puffy.

"Do you wanna talk about what happened?" I asked, slowly drawing out each word and testing her reaction.

She shrugged, not smiling, unlike how she was earlier in the day. She didn't have the same warmth in her eyes. I felt compelled to speak my mind. "Well, what he did was really shitty. I think you should tell somebody, get him put in jail. That's really awful that a dad—"

"Andy, stop," she said, cutting my rant short. "I love my dad. He might be really shit at being a parent sometimes, but…" she let out a short huff, "nevermind."

I was at a loss for words, so I just said, "I'm listening."

She snorted and wiped her tears away again. "Well, uh," she held out her forearm, "I got a tattoo." she laughed.

On the underside of her arm was a depiction of a scale etched out in black ink.

"I could never get a tattoo," I said.

"Oh. Well, anyway," Max said, ignoring my comment, "so, Daenan and I are really into zodiacs, well more me, but anyway, I got it a while ago and my dad hasn't been around much, so he didn't notice, but he was home when I got back today. He wanted to spend time with me, I guess. He saw it and he started bitching at me, saying I'm too young and shit, but, like, it's none of his business." She started to shake a bit. "So I told him to fuck off. We were in the kitchen and he was all like, 'Look what you did. That doesn't go away, Maxine.' And he pulled on my arm." She shrugged as if to say it couldn't be helped. "I hit my head on a kitchen cabinet."

I couldn't help but feel bad for her. My dad certainly never acted like that and I'd never been hit before either, except by Tony when we were rough housing or fighting over the tv remote. I hummed, signaling for her to continue.

She pursed her lips. "My dad was really mad, so I wanted to, like, let him cool off, you know? But I couldn't go to Daenan's house 'cause he's still pissed at me or whatever, and none of my other friends live around here, so yeah."

I knew I should have been more focused on comforting her, but that piqued my curiosity. I couldn't help remembering the confusing scene at Daenan's apartment. "Yeah…why's he mad at you anyway?"

She rolled her eyes. "'Cause he's stupid. He has a crush on me and he's acting all crazy. He thinks that just because I *tease* him (she put 'tease' in air quotes), I should have to be his girlfriend. So, he's being a huge dick about it."

I hummed again, this time out of deep curiosity. I wondered if she kissed everyone like she kissed me.

"Let's go to sleep now," I said. I leaned over and turned the light out again. "Goodnight."

Chapter 3

I woke up to a screeching sound. I opened my eyes, slightly irritated. A little girl was staring back at me. A week had passed since we had arrived in Nevada and I was beginning to tire from the constant pandemonium of children running around throwing barbies and legos. I sighed. "Hi, Josie."

"Andy?" she said.

"Yes, Josie?" She had a way of asking permission before asking a question.

"Will you play barbies with me?"

"I got stuff to do," I said, pulling off the covers and swinging my legs over the bed.

I got dressed and headed into the living room; with Josie following close behind.

Tony was sitting on the floor with Tyler, a skinny red-headed boy who resembled

Chuckie from *Rugrats.* He was the middle child of three, but he never told me how old he was. In fact, he didn't speak much at all. They were building a puzzle on the coffee table. "Where's mom?" I asked.

Tony looked up at me. "I think she went to the store."

Darla was in the kitchen, undoubtedly making macaroni and cheese for the shitlings. The phone rang and Darla answered with, "What?"

Meanwhile, ten-year-old David, the oldest of the three, had taken Josie's barbie and was making her jump for it. "Give her back!" Josie squealed, reaching on her tiptoes. David was pretty tall for his age and in contrast to his siblings. He laughed giddily.

"David Donald Larson! Give your sister her doll right now," Darla commanded. He dropped the barbie, ran through the dining room so he was out of the reach of his mother and shouted, "I hope you step on a Lego!"

She rolled her eyes. "No. You don't get them until next weekend," Darla said sternly before pressing the phone against her shoulder so whoever was on the other line couldn't hear. "Andy, honey, could you and Tony take those kids down to the park for a bit?"

"Um..." I said reluctantly, "sure."

"Thanks, hun." She put the phone back up to her ear. "Fine! You can come get 'em then!"

Tony and I gathered up the kids and got out of there as quickly as we could.

"Hi, Andy," I heard a familiar voice say. I looked up, shielding my eyes from the sun. I could barely make out the image of Max smiling down at me. I looked over at Tony, who was sitting next to me on the park bench, as if to say, *scram*.

"I'm gonna go play with the kids," Tony said, getting up and walking away.

I looked back up at Max. "What's up?"

She shifted slightly so she was now blocking the sun. I could see that her black eye had finally healed. I wondered how she was coping at home with her dad. We hadn't seen each other since that night.

"Nothing much..." she replied.

"Oh. Cool."

Just then, Josie came running up. "Andy! Look what I made!"

"I'm busy," I said, shooing her with my hand, but not looking to see what she was talking about.

"Andy!" Josie whined. "Tony showed me how to make a daisy chain."

"Josie," I said sternly, turning to face her, "I'm busy. Leave me alone."

She ran off, seemingly unfazed.

Max bit her lip. "I was wondering... would you like to go out sometime?" She gave me a big toothy smile.

"What?" I felt myself jolt back. Did she just ask me on a date? Is she just assuming that I like girls? I don't. I found myself in a panic. "Ah, uh, I'm sorry, I can't."

"Oh," said Max, making a face that showed she was almost as surprised as I was. However, that face was quickly replaced with sad eyes and an artificial smile. "I just thought we could go see a movie or something."

I looked out at Tony, who was playing out on the jungle gym with David and Tyler, to see if he was aware of our conversation, but he obviously had his hands full.

"Look, I don't care what you thought," I said, feeling a little heated, "but I'm not like that, okay?"

"Okay." Her brow dropped into a dramatic scowl.

I was shocked at my behavior towards her, but I wasn't about to correct it and make her think I was revoking my statement. I couldn't deal with something like that. "I'm sorry," I said, quickly changing the subject. "Where's Josie?"

My eyes darted over to the jungle gym again. There was Tony, David, and Tyler. I started to panic. "Oh shit! Where *is* Josie?"

"She was just here a minute ago..." Max's voice trailed off. She stood there frozen for a second and raised a nearly limp hand to point in the direction of the bathrooms. "She's over there."

Josie stood there smiling and laughing in her little summer dress. Above her stood a man, who looked to be around thirty, wearing an oversized vest, white t-shirt, and big wire-rimmed glasses. He leaned down, putting his hands on his knees so that he could speak face to face with her.

"Josie…" I hollered, as Max and I jogged over to her.

She looked up at me and smiled.

"How are you doing, miss?" He asked in a slight rasp, much like that of a smoker, and offered me a hand to shake. I opened my mouth, but couldn't think of anything to say. Something was off. I glanced over at Max. She looked concerned.

"I'm okay," I said and looked down at Josie. "We're going home soon. You should come play for a while before we go." I took her by the hand and led her away. Tony was watching us as we came over to him. Tony hopped down from the structure to greet us as Josie joined her brothers.

"Who was that?" Tony asked.

"No one," I said, still feeling a little sheepish.

Max touched my arm. "Andy…" she said with eyes like a deer in headlights, "I'm going home. I think you should too."

"Oh…okay." I said a little confused. "Is everything okay with your dad?"

"I'll be fine," she replied, dismissing my question. Then she ran off.

Tony and I hurried back to the house with the kids, but were stopped at the yard by the sight of a man storming out of the front door.

"I can't believe you!" the man shouted as he ran out.

Darla stood in the doorway watching. As the man got closer he seemed to notice us for the first time. He froze, looking down at Tyler, David and little Josie.

"Daddy?" Josie said timidly.

"Hey sweetie." The man smiled and swooped her up in his arms. "You wanted to see daddy right?"

Josie looked more confused. "Yes..."

He scoffed.

"Hello," I said trying to ease the tension, "I'm Andy...Is everything okay?"

He frowned, putting Josie down. Darla called the kids inside. "Yeah... just some custody issues, I guess. Nice to meet you."

He walked out to the old rusty station wagon that was sitting next to the house. I could hear the car door screech as he opened it. He looked at the house for a moment and finally drove away.

Chapter 4

It was Sunday morning and the kids had gone to their dad's house for the weekend. Mom was cooking pancakes—a long forgotten Sunday tradition—and was trying to make small talk with Tony and I. Since we (or at least, I) had been avoiding her since we'd arrived, I suppose that was her attempt at repairing some of the damage she'd done.

"What have you been doing these last couple of weeks?" my mother teased. "I've barely seen you."

"Well, " I said casually, "I've been hanging out with Max a lot."

"Hm...who's Max? I don't really feel comfortable with you running around with some boy I haven't met," Mom said, adding in her unsolicited opinion.

"She's a girl," Tony jumped in.

"Oh." My mom chuckled. "Never mind then. You should invite her over for dinner sometime."

"Yeah. Sure," I said, rolling my eyes.

"Hey sweetie, I'm gonna be out today... job hunting. I thought it would be fun if Darla took you and Tony clothes shopping." She smiled excitedly. "You two could use some summer clothes."

Tony lifted his attention from the massive stack of pancakes on his plate. "That sounds cool."

Oh great, I thought, *I have to spend the day with Darla*. "It's not like we live here," I muttered under my breath. I didn't think my mom heard me.

"How 'bout it honey?" I shuddered at Darla's voice behind me, the pitch of it rattling my ear drum.

She came into the kitchen and poured herself a cup of coffee, while a wide grin spread across her cheeks.

"Yeah, sounds fun." I wasn't sure if I was glaring at her or not, but I didn't care either way.

I wasn't looking forward to spending the day with Darla. Even before the events of the previous week, I had found her rather bothersome to be around (she was a little too bubbly for my taste, and her southern accent and pageant girl positivity made me want to strangle her). Normally, I was able to forgive such irritating character traits if I felt that a person had other redeemable qualities, but ignoring those traits in her was a bigger challenge than with most other people.

Still, when Darla had said we were going to the mall, I had gotten a little excited. I hadn't been shopping in a long time (Mom didn't like malls because they were 'littered with distractions') and I was in dire need of an escape from this whole small town experience for a while. Unfortunately, my excitement quickly turned to disappointment when I realized that when Darla said mall, she actually meant strip mall. We wound up at Payless to pick out shoes before heading over to Ross.

"Tony," Darla said sweetly, "why don't you go pick out some t-shirts and meet us at the dressing rooms?"

"Okay."

"So…" she started, "do you have a boyfriend?"

"No," I replied shortly, shifting through the hangers on a rack.

"Aw, that's a shame. You're such a pretty girl."

I tried to figure out what her angle was, but was drawing a blank. "I guess so."

"Your birthday's comin' up soon, in't it?" She asked, a smile appearing on her face.

"Yeah?" I replied, feeling weary.

She beamed. "Well, how 'bout we find you a cute lil' birthday dress?"

I grimaced, not trying very hard to hide my objection to the idea. "Uh…I don't really wear dresses." There was the angle. Of course she wanted to play dress up. She wanted me to be her pretty little doll. *I'll have you know I'm not a pageant girl, Darla.*

Despite my protests, she began rifling through the clothing racks and shoving garments at me until they were heaped high enough in my arms that I had to stretch my neck to see over the top of them. Then, she proceeded to force me into a dressing room where I reluctantly began to try them on. I tossed aside the dresses that were either too child-like, too feminine, or too gaudy, before finding a decent one: a simple light green dress that ended at the knee and had a little lace on the hem.

"Can I see?" Darla called into the dressing room.

I opened the door.

She gasped. "That's adorable! With a little makeup, you'd be a knockout."

That made me smile a little. I did look good, I supposed. People had always told me how attractive I was, but I guess I never took those compliments to heart. "My mom says makeup is for girls that are…" I motioned air quotes, "busy."

She snorted, "There's nothin' wrong with a lil' lipstick."

"Darla…" I started timidly, "why are you helping my mom?"

She frowned. "Oh, I don't know." She paused. "I guess it's 'cause I know what it's like to be cheated on."

"But they could still be a good person? If they cheated, I mean," I asked, remembering the day I'd discovered my father's affair.

It was a few months before the end of the school year. My mom had taken my brother to a doctor's appointment and I had just gotten home from school.

I kicked off my shoes and tossed my backpack on the couch as I came in. My dad's car was in the driveway, so I assumed he had a client over and was discussing a case. I ran upstairs, planning to go hang out in my room, but as I passed my dad's office, I heard laughter, a woman's laugh.

"Dad?" I said as I opened the door.

"Andrea!" My dad quickly buttoned his pants while the petite blonde girl who was propped up on his desk attempted to hide her flesh (which was already pretty well covered with tattoos).

I bolted out into the hallway with him following close behind.

"Andrea, sweetie, she's just a client from work. Nothing's going on," he pleaded.

I couldn't keep from laughing. "Bullshit, nothing's going on. So she's a criminal, huh? That's great." I began to walk away, but he grabbed my arm.

"Please don't say anything to your mom. I just gotta figure things out." The look he gave me was pathetic, like that of a stray mutt, not a powerful defense attorney.

I pulled away. "Sure, whatever."

Darla rubbed her lips together, thinking about my question for a moment. "Maybe. All I know is that if you catch a man cheatin', that's a look at his character."

When I got back to the house, mom was preparing dinner. It was as if she thought her cooking would make things feel more normal. Tony and I started to head for our room as Darla went to sit at the counter with mom.

"Andy, " mom said, smiling, "come here a sec."

"What?" I asked, apathetically.

She proceeded to chop celery. "Nicole called my cell. You should give her a call back," she gestured to her purse.

"Oh," I said, caught a little off guard. "Okay, I will." I said this as I grabbed the phone and stepped outside.

Nicole had been my best friend since middle school. With all that had been going on over the last two weeks, I had nearly forgotten about her. She was probably royally pissed by now; we didn't usually go more than a few days without communicating in some form.

"Hello?" Nicole chirped.

"Hi," I said, slightly hesitant. I had almost forgotten about my life back home and wasn't sure how my new life fit in or what Nicole would think of my adventures. "It's Andy," I said with a smile.

"Duh!" she squawked, "Where have you been? I haven't heard from you in like two weeks. We need to hang out. We should go to the mall. I went to your house, but no one came to the door. Is someone staying with you? 'Cause this car has been parked outside your house for like three days and I thought it was a little...urban, for your mom's taste. Or did you finally get a car? If so, I really think—"

"Nicole," I cut her off, "that's not my car."

"Oh." She paused. "Then who's—"

"I don't know," I said, hoping my scowl didn't appear in my voice.

She replied with a drawn out, "okay," and continued, "...so, do you want to go to the mall? I just got paid and I wanna get some new jeans. I can pick you up in a few."

I sighed. "Nicole, I gotta tell you something."

"Okay? Shoot."

I pondered a moment over how to put it into words. The complexity of the situation was something I felt Nicole wouldn't quite grasp. And besides that, there was the matter of what she would say, not to mention who she would tell. "I moved."

"Crap! No way. Where?"

"Nevada..." I hesitated, "I don't know if I'm coming back anytime soon."

There was a pause. I assumed Nicole was thinking of the appropriate way to respond, but her response was surprisingly casual. "I'm sorry. I'm gonna call Brittany and see if she wants to go to the mall."

"Brittany?"

I remembered last year's Easter picnic. The tables outside the church were decorated with different pastels and images of white rabbits and chicks hatching from eggs. The younger kids scavenged the church yard, trying to collect as many colored eggs as possible. I watched them, remembering when I was younger, how I always ended up collecting more eggs than I could carry in my basket. I was faster than the boys and more observant than the girls. Although, now that I was older, I didn't understand why I wanted to collect the eggs in the first place. For candy?

"Whatcha thinkin' about, Andy?" said a familiar voice from behind me.

I smiled. Justin always paid more attention to me than other people did. Our families had been friends since we were babies and we sort of grew up alongside each other.

"Nothing." I turned to face him.

He dropped his jaw. "Wow!"

"What?"

"Oh nothing, you just look freaking adorable today." He grinned mischievously.

I noted my worn out overalls and faded blue t-shirt.

I chuckled. "Yeah, sure," I said, and punched him playfully.

"No, really," he insisted, "but you always look adorable."

"Thanks, " I said, flattered, but slightly uncomfortable. I looked around. "You don't need to…"

Nicole waved at me frantically as she came from the church parking lot, holding a bowl of some kind of salad in her other hand. Great timing.

"There's Nicole," I said, giving a slight smile, and jogging over to her, happy to have an excuse to escape Justin.

She was all done up, like she was every Sunday for church, with loose blonde curls, and a floral dress that moved as she did.

She pouted. "I thought you were going to wear a dress."

I shrugged. "Yeah, well I didn't find one in time. Let's go sit."

Not long after we had sat down, Brittany approached. She had a petite frame,a round face and long hair that she always kept in a braid. Her and her family had moved to our neighborhood just a few weeks before the school year started and I didn't know her very well.

She grinned at me. "May I talk to you?"

I followed her away from the picnic tables. "What's up?"

"Stop hanging all over Justin, okay?" she said abruptly.

I laughed. "What?"

"Don't play dumb. I saw you flirting with him," she said.

"Oh." I laughed again. "I can assure you, I have no interest in Justin. We're just friends."

She hummed. "Is that so? Then why is it I don't see you with any other boys?"

"Well that's not really any of your business, is it?" I said, getting a little annoyed.

"Oh I see." She smirked. "You don't like boys, do you?"

I balled up my fist, trying to keep from losing my temper. "Look, I respect that he's your boyfriend or whatever, and I don't have any interest in him or any other boy for that matter. I don't know what you're trying to do, but leave me alone."

I started to walk away, but her voice stopped me. "Well I'm obligated to tell Pastor Dan."

I turned and faced her. She continued, "The youth group camping trip is coming up and it would be very inappropriate for a..." she drew the word out, pronouncing each vowel and consonant, "…*lesbian* to be in a tent with sleeping girls."

I could barely breathe. I felt as if my heart had stopped. "What's your problem?" I stuttered.

She smirked. "I don't like you. You think you're better than everyone, but you're not. You're fake."

I stumbled away from her without saying a word. I felt like I was going to puke; I was sure I looked it. I sat down quietly next to Nicole, but she didn't seem to notice any change in my mood.

The next night, while we were all eating dinner, my mother received a phone call. She got up from the table to answer it.

"Hello?" she said.

There was a pause.

"A concern? What type of concern?" she asked as a look of confusion spread over her face. She paused again and frowned. "I assure you my daughter is of no concern of yours or anyone else there."

There was another pause, then my mother raised her voice slightly, "Well I suggest you question your source," and hung up the phone.

Everyone at the table had been sitting in silence, with my father and brother both staring at my mom. Tony continued to eat quietly while dad and I had stopped to listen. My mother wiped sweat away from her forehead. "Andy, sweetie, when you finish eating, I would like to see you upstairs."

I nodded and mouthed a silent, "Okay."

I wasn't really able to eat much after that, as I was getting that sick feeling in my stomach again. So, I pushed my food around a bit, cleared my plate, and went upstairs.

"Mom?" I called down the hall.

"I'm in here," she called back from my parents' bedroom.

She was folding laundry. As I came in, she set down the towel she was folding. "Andy, I'm afraid I have some bad news. Pastor Dan called and he said that you will not be able to attend the youth campout this year. Is there something you want to tell me?"

I crossed my arms. "No."

She arched her back, like she always did when she was nervous. "Apparently, one of the other parents told Pastor Dan that..." she lowered her voice to a whisper "...you are confused about your sexuality. Is that true? If it is, we'll help you...we can send you to counseling, if you need it. There are—"

"No!" I snapped, throwing my arms down. "God, mom! No."

She backed off. "Okay...so what's going on then?"

"It's Brittany," I said, crossing my arms again. "She hates me."

"Why?"

I rolled my eyes. "I don't know. She's

a stupid teenage girl. I'm going to bed."

The memory left me a little dazed. "Brittany?"

"Yeah...so?" Nicole said. "We've been hanging out a lot more lately. I didn't think you would mind."

"Well, I do mind," I said, grinding my teeth together.

Nicole grunted. "Get over it already. I mean seriously, grow up. It's not that big a deal."

"It is a big deal!" I yelled and hung up the phone.

I went back out into the kitchen to hand the phone to my mom. She was putting the last of the ingredients into a pot. I put it back in my mom's purse and was about to go back to mine and Tony's room when she said, "I was thinking... your birthday's coming up. Why don't we throw you a little party? We could—"

"No."

She looked disappointed. "Why not? We could invite a few friends and get a cake..."

I locked eyes with her. "I don't have any friends."

She frowned, wiping off her hands. "What about that girl? What was her name? Ah, Max. What about her?"

"We barely know each other," I said, not willing to budge. "I'm going for a walk."

Before my mother could say no, I went

out the front door, and into the hot summer night.

Chapter 6

I hated the desert; I loved trees, and the smell of rain, splashing through puddles, and how it was never completely quiet. I hated the desert, but I found that the more I walked, I actually had more freedom than I ever desired. I could just keep walking and there was nothing to distract me from my thoughts, at least for the first half hour.

Once I passed under the sign that read, "The Biggest Little City in the World," I knew I was downtown, where the tall buildings on either side of the street doused the sidewalk with a glow from half-lit neon signs; and scraggly vagrants milled about, asking passers-by for money. One particularly unkempt man approached me, and I politely told him I had no cash.

Other shadowy figures passed by,

avoiding my gaze, sometimes tossing a cigarette butt or spitting on the sidewalk. I continued walking until I came to a flashing sign that read, "Arcade," and ducked inside.

It must have been around 9 p.m. by the time I found the arcade , because it was starting to get dark and there were only a few lonely looking people left inside, probably trying to beat the top scores or use up the last of their tokens. I walked down an aisle of gaming machines, passing unoccupied racing games and Miss Pacman screens. I turned the corner and that's when I saw a familiar figure.

With broad shoulders draped over an old Asteroids machine and the scorpion tattoo on his neck, it was unmistakably Daenan. He didn't seem to notice me beside him. "Daenen..." I said softly. He jumped and turned his head to face me, "What?!" In the same instant, the dreaded "Game Over" text appeared on the screen.

He sighed. "What do you want?"

"Nothing..." I said, unsure of what to say, "...I just..."

The corners of his mouth lifted a bit, as if to resemble a smile. "Oh, you're Max's friend."

"Sort of. My name's Andy, you know?" I reminded him, slightly annoyed.

"I know. What are you doing out here anyway?" he asked flatly.

I looked at him, blank faced. "I could ask you the same thing."

"Whatever." He started to walk away. I let him go, before I remembered how intimidating the scene was outside. "Wait," I said. He turned around to face me. "I need help getting home."

He nodded. "All right."

I thought it would've taken more effort to convince him. He proceeded to walk outside and I followed closely behind. I felt rather pathetic, but I wasn't sure I'd be able to make it home safely on my own. He was quieter than when we first met; perhaps my first impression wasn't the norm.

He paid no attention to me, but he slowed down a bit so I could keep up with him. I stared up to his stone-faced expression. "Why are you out by yourself anyway?" he said, still not looking at me.

"I've been angry a lot lately, and I guess I just...wanted to leave, so I started walking," I said.

He raised an eyebrow at me. "Why were you angry?"

"It's a long story," I replied.

He made a little, "Hmm," and looked back at the street.

I kicked a pebble at my feet. "My mom moved us out here...unexpectedly and my birthday is coming up soon, and my mom wants to throw me a party that I have no one to invite to. I just don't want to be *that* girl anymore. I'm so sick of everything!"

"What kind of girl were you?" he asked.

I thought about that a moment and said, "Perfect."

He scoffed.

I continued, "…Always doing what I was told, going to church, getting good grades, playing soccer…never saying what I think."

He chuckled. "That doesn't sound perfect to me," he said as his face returned to a resting scowl. "So, fuck it."

"Is that what you do? Fuck it? Do whatever you want?" I asked.

"Well, no one gives a shit what I do." He paused. "So, yeah, in a way."

We were quiet for a while until we got away from all the motels and neon lights. My curiosity about him was growing more and more.

"Are you and Max close?" I asked, hesitantly.

"Sort of…" he replied, "we grew up together." He opened his mouth as if to say something and closed it again, before adding, "She likes you, you know?"

I felt my face getting hot. "I know…"

I remembered the day Daenan and I had met, when Max brought me to his apartment. "She likes you though," I said.

"No," he said abruptly, "she likes playing with me."

I searched his face for any sign of

emotion, but found nothing. "Do you resent her?"

There it was. He looked quickly at his shoes and straight ahead again. He didn't answer the question, instead asking, "How old are you?"

"Seventeen."

He smiled wickedly. "Have you ever had a drink?"

"No..." I started, "my parents never let us, but I'm not legal anyway. Why'd you ask how old I am?"

"Just wondering. Wanna go to a party with me tomorrow night?" he said, staring at me, suddenly looking excited for the first time in the night.

I thought about it a minute and smiled. "Okay."

I stumbled into the house, exhausted from the night's journey and was greeted by my mother who had been waiting up for me in the living room. She scowled, pointing up at the clock on the wall. It was about 1:10 a.m..

"Where in God's name have you been?" she started.

"Mom I—"

She cut me off, "Do you have any idea what time it is? You can't just leave without telling me where you're going," she continued on and on until I finally couldn't take it anymore.

"Mom!" I shouted.

She stopped talking, and tapped her

foot rapidly against the floor.

"I'm sorry," I said, not really meaning it. I just wanted the nagging to end.

She scoffed. "Well, *I'm sorry* doesn't cut it. You're grounded."

I should have expected as much. "For how long?"

Her face softened. "We'll see. Get yourself to bed."

Chapter 6

I slept in and when I woke up, the house was quiet. I got dressed and wandered into the living room where my brother was sitting on the couch, holding an issue of Spiderman in his hands.

"Comic books?" I said. "Better than porn, I suppose."

"Shut up," Tony said with a scowl, blushing only slightly and shifting in his seat. I spotted a pencil eraser poking up from the pages.

"Are you drawing something?" I snatched the comic book from him and a paper that had been wedged between the pages fell out onto the floor.

"Hey!" he protested, trying to grab the paper before I could, but he wasn't fast enough.

I examined it. On the paper, there were several sketches of Spiderman and the Green Goblin in different actions and positions.

"What is this?" I asked, handing his things back to him.

"I just wanted to see if I could draw them."

"Did you trace?"

"No," he said, sounding slightly defensive, "I just copied the poses."

I rustled his hair. "Well, they're really good."

"Don't touch me!" he growled, "God!"

I started to walk into the kitchen.

"Andy?" he said.

"What?"

"Do you think I should take a drawing class?" he asked in a small voice.

I couldn't help smiling. "Yeah, definitely."

I ate breakfast and joined Tony in the living room, dropping myself into the recliner with a thud.

I yawned dramatically. "So bored!"

"Why don't you go somewhere?" Tony suggested, not looking up from what he was drawing.

"Can't. I'm grounded for going on that walk last night."

"That sucks," my brother empathized to the best of his ability. "Watch TV then."

So I spent the remainder of the day watching reality television and eagerly awaiting the night's festivities.

I laid on my bed, already dressed in Doc Martens and shorts. I wasn't too worried that Tony would notice, because his face was buried in yet another comic—and he was a boy, after all. I heard a light tap at the window and sprang to my feet. It was Max. Daenan was there too, standing a few feet away.

"Are you ready?"

I grinned so wide that my cheeks hurt. "Yup."

Tony whipped his head around. "What? Where are you going?"

I put a finger to my lips. "Shhhhh...just out."

"You gotta let me come too," he said in a low voice, "or I'm telling." He grinned devilishly, waiting for my response.

"Fine," I said, "you can come."

I looked back to Max. "I'm sorry, but my brother's coming too."

"That's fine."

I swung my legs over the windowsill and hopped down. Tony followed. Daenan scanned my body. I was pleased to have the attention. He knitted his brows, as if he didn't like that I'd noticed him looking at me.

Max was dressed a lot more provocatively than I was. She wore tight skinny jeans and a top that was loose enough that it slunked off of her shoulders, exposing her bra; she seemed to be determined to show off what little breast tissue she had.

"Let's go!" she said, bouncing with excitement.

The house was located in a nicer, more affluent part of town. It was tall with enormous beveled windows, partially hidden beneath stone arches. Daenan opened the door and walked in unannounced. We followed close behind. Inside it was dimly lit and mostly quiet. We were standing in a large entryway. The kitchen was on the left, and in front of us was a tall wooden staircase with a dark wrought iron railing. To the right was a long hallway. We could hear laughter coming from that direction. Max led us, skipping down the hallway, and as we got closer to the room at the end of it, I could smell the pungent odor of weed. Entering the doorway, there were three steps that led down into a sitting room with big fluffy couches and glass end tables.

"Brady!" Max waved vigorously at a boy in a letterman's jacket who was sitting alone on one of the couches. He laughed, which accentuated his droopy eyes. "Hey," he said, standing up. She hugged him and gave him a gentle peck as she pulled away. He showed that stupid stoner smile again and Max sat next to him on the couch.

Tony reviewed his surroundings with wide eyes. Brady, surprisingly, caught his stare. "Sit down bro," Brady said.

Tony scanned the room for his options. A girl with blonde hair smiled at him, then sat up straight, pushing her boobs into the air. His face turned scarlet. "Come on," she whined, "I don't bite." Tony looked at me, asking permission with his eyes. I smirked, a signal that it was fine, and he sat right between her and a brunette with freckles. The brunette pulled down her skirt and shifted her weight as Tony sat down.

Max was hanging on Brady, running a hand up and down his leg. He had broad shoulders and a noticeable stomach, but was still relatively attractive with his short curly hair and a beard that lined his jaw. I looked at Daenan. His face had twisted into a rather sour position.

Max, whispered something into Brady's ear, then quickly got up from the couch. "Don't wait up, okay?" She gave Daenan a quick kiss on the cheek and disappeared down the hall.

Daenan shook his head,. "Got anything to drink?"

"There's some beer in the kitchen," said the brunette.

I hopped up onto the kitchen counter and Daenan handed me a beer before getting one for himself.

"Here goes my first drink." I raised my can in the air.

He watched me as I took a big swig, and nearly spit it out. "That's awful!" I laughed, sticking out my tongue for effect. "Bleh."

He chuckled. "Just drink it. You gotta wait for the buzz."

I finished it. He handed me another and I finished that one as well. "Okay… I feel a lot better now."

"See? I told ya."

"I don't wanna go back out there," I said. "My brother's probably having a threeway with those girls."

"Good for him!"

I shuddered. "Ew," I said while getting down from the counter and stepping closer to Daenan.

"What are you looking at?"

I pointed at his tattoo. "Did you get that for Max?"

He covered it with his hand. "No, I uh… well, I guess so, but not like that."

"Not like what?"

"You know…well, I got it 'cause she asked me to, she said," Daenan said, doing his best impression of Max. "It'll be like blood brothers. Only without disease."

"Hmmm… okay." I looked at him for a moment. "Your eyes are green," I said.

"So?"

"Nothing, I just never noticed that before."

It was obvious that he wasn't feeling the effects of the alcohol like I was. At that moment I thought about what it would be like to kiss him. He seemed like a nice enough guy. Impulsively, I pulled his face down to mine and kissed him. He rested one hand on my hip and the other gently caressed my arm. After a few seconds, he pulled away, leaving his hand on my hip, but taking a small step back.

"Andy..." he spoke slowly, as if he were thinking hard, "this isn't a good time to explore feelings between us."

"What?" I felt as if he had just uttered some foreign language. "What feelings?"

It felt like the tone of the conversation had shifted for both of us. I hated it when people made assumptions about me. Who was he to try to get into my head? He had no right to me. But as I looked at the serious expression on his face, I could feel that I hurt him.

"I'm sorry." I tried my best to ignore the rage I was feeling and put it aside. "You're right."

We looked at each other for a moment. "Wait," I said, as something occurred to me. "Are you attracted to me?" I asked, fairly sure of the answer.

He blinked, letting go of me and taking a step back. "I guess...sorta."

I guess? Sorta? Is he for real?

"Okay, fine," I said, backing away from him. "I wonder if Max is back yet."

"Andy, look I just don—" he started.

"I said it's fine. Okay?" I responded a little louder than I intended.

He hung his head. "Okay."

I shoved at him playfully. "Come on. Let's go see what everyone's doing."

Tony didn't notice us when we came in. His eyes were locked on the blonde girl; her hand was on his knee, and the brunette had scooted as far away from them as she could without actually leaving the couch. She smiled at us as we came in, probably relieved that she was no longer a third wheel. Daenan and I sat down on the other sofa.

"Is Max still…" I started.

Tony and the blonde both spun their heads around, apparently finally aware we had returned. Tony scooted away from her.

"Yeah," replied the brunette in a small voice.

Everyone was quiet. The blonde picked at her fingernails and everyone else just sat quietly. All of a sudden, she shot up from the couch. "Let's play truth or dare!"

The suggestion was met with some reluctance, but no real opposition, with most everyone in the room responding with "sure."

"I'm Rachel, by the way. What's your name?" she asked, pointing in my direction.

"Andy."

"Okay, Andy…truth or dare?"

"Truth," I said without hesitating.

"Lame…okay…are you hooking up with

Daenan?"

"No," I replied, my response flat. I pointed at the brunette. "You."

"Hailey," she corrected me while shifting her weight. "Um...I don't know..." she gave a small smile and shrugged, "dare, I guess."

"Hmm...I dare you to...kiss the next person who walks into the room."

Rachel glared at me.

Just then, Max appeared in the doorway with a huge smile on her face. "Hey guys," she said.

Brady nodded. "Sup."

Hailey started to go white. "I can't."

"Can't what?" Max said, tilting her head.

"You don't have to," Rachel said abruptly. "It's a stupid game anyway."

I rolled my eyes. "Whatever."

She got up from her seat, her hands in fists. "You can't expect her to kiss a lesbian! That's gross!"

Hailey shifted in her seat, her eyes locked on Max.

"I'm not a lesbian," Max said, still tipping her head as if looking at a strange creature, but evidently catching on quickly.

Rachel ignored Max, her eyes still locked on me. She turned red in the face and looked as though she would begin foaming at the mouth any minute.

"She probably has mouth herpes anyway," Rachel said, whipping her head around while shooting a quick glare at Max. "Faggot."

Hailey sat on the couch, running a strand of hair through her fingers.

Daenan took a quick step toward the girls, his veins bulging from his neck. "What'd you say?"

"I hate to break it to you, but your friend is a *whore!*" Rachel yelled the word "whore", not shaken by Daenan's stance.

"Says you," I said, pointing at her. "You were all over my brother. You know he's fourteen right?"

As I said this, Tony sidestepped away from her.

Brady sighed, obviously still very stoned. "Woah..." His eyes darted around the room. We all waited to see if he had anything valuable to say, but all that came out of his mouth was, "uh..."

"We're leaving," Rachel announced, yanking Hailey up off the couch by her arm.

"Ow! That hurts," Hailey whined and was once again ignored.

They passed by Max on their way out. She stopped them with her words, "Hailey, we should hangout more often. You remember how to get to my apartment, right?"

Almost instantaneously, Rachel spun on her toes and slapped Max across the face. The clapping sound echoed through the house. The girls stood there for a moment, staring at us. I shoved at Rachel's shoulders, pushing her back. "Go!" I commanded, and they left.

Chapter 7

Everyone was silent. Max stood there with her eyes closed. She lifted a hand and pressed it against her reddened cheek. She opened her eyes, blinking a few times, and staggered towards Daenan. He wrapped his arms around her and held her for an uncomfortable length of time.

She stepped away, touching her cheek again, and then a wide grin formed on her face. "That was fun," she said with a laugh "I love parties. It's really late though."

Tony and Daenan looked just as confused as I felt. Brady just looked high.

She danced over to him with her usual high energy, kissed him on the cheek and said, "Thanks for inviting me."

We scurried out of the house as if we

were fleeing a crime scene. On our walk home, Max and I let the boys hang back so they could talk about Tony's experience with the girls. I didn't really care to know about my young brother's conquests.

"What do you think of Brady?" Max cooed and took a puff off a joint that she apparently had been saving in her pocket.

I thought about that a minute. I had never had that much interest in guys like him. I hung around with those kinds of people back home, and they didn't interest me.

I responded with, "If you like that sort of thing."

She tilted her head. "What do you mean?"

I shrugged. "He's just a little too Abercrombie for me."

She snorted. "Aren't you Abercrombie?"

"Not anymore."

I turned around to face Tony and Daenan and walked backwards, temporarily shunning Max for her comment. A smile formed on Tony's face. "Those girls liked me."

We all laughed. Daenan punched him playfully. Daenan was actually really cute when he wasn't being such an ass. The kiss flashed back into my mind. I couldn't help comparing it to Max's. When Max kissed me, it was exciting, but when I kissed Daenan, it was so much more comfortable.

"What?" he said, looking at me with bug eyes.

I realized that I was grinning at him like an idiot. I felt my face getting hot again. "Nothing."

Tony and Max were both staring at us. Max looked back and forth between the two of us as if trying to find an invisible thread connecting our heads. "What's up with you guys?"

"Nothing," Daenan said quickly.

"What are you talking about?" I added.

She shrugged. "Whatever."

When we reached Darla's house, everything seemed normal. The lights were out and I couldn't hear any activity inside. I was relieved that they didn't seem to notice we were gone. I had left the window open so that Tony and I could climb back inside. Tony hoisted himself up and into the bedroom. I followed.

"Goodnight," Max said. I gave her and Daenan a small wave and closed the window.

Tony and I quickly changed into our pajamas and I tucked myself into bed as if I had been there the whole time.

Chapter 8

The next evening, I walked myself over to the apartments where Max and Daenan lived. I went to apartment number 16B and knocked on the door. I stood there, rising up and down on my toes as I waited. Finally, the door opened.

"Hey Andy," Max said with a big grin on her face. "What's up?"

"My mom told me I should invite you to dinner tonight."

"Sweet!" she responded with enough enthusiasm for both of us. "Come inside. I gotta get my shoes."

The inside of the apartment was dark except for the light coming in through the kitchen windows, and it smelled like musty laundry. Max disappeared into a bedroom. "Bye, Dad. I'll be back later. Love you," I heard her say in the other room.

She came out. "Okay. I'm ready."

The dining room was filled with the sounds of silverware clinking and scraping against dinner plates as we pretended to eat our food. Due to the lack of conversation, the empty space acted like a sound vacuum, which produced an awkward pressure that was too much to withstand.

My mother cleared her throat. "So... Max, what does your father do?"

Max stared at her as if she were speaking a foreign language.

"For work?" my mother added.

Max sat up straight, smoothing out her Blood on The Dance Floor t-shirt. "Ah, he used to work in a factory, making security systems...but he got laid off a while ago, so he's unemployed right now..."

My mom smiled as if she had tasted something sour. "I'm sure things will look up."

"So..." she said changing the subject, "Tony says the three of you met at the park."

I widened my eyes at Tony and pursed my lips together. He gave a subtle nod.

"Yeah," Max responded.

"That sounds fun," said my mother, trying to sound as if she were enjoying the conversation. "What else have you kids been doing for fun? You've been out quite a bit."

Max started to open her mouth, but I jumped in and said, "Just watching Netflix and stuff."

She tilted her head, "Well, maybe if you explore a little more, you'll find some things to do."

There was a silence.

"Ah," she said, suddenly thinking of a topic, "Andy's going to college in Denver in the fall. Are you planning on going to school?"

Max cleared her throat. "Well, I'm not done with high school yet."

"Oh, how old are you?"

"Nineteen..."

My mom narrowed her eyes and pressed her lips together, not saying anything. I assumed she was waiting for Max to elaborate.

She gritted her teeth in a smile. "Uh... well, I dropped out when I was fifteen... I'm planning on going to Job Corps soon though."

After dinner, Max helped me with the dishes in the kitchen while Tony and my mother went to build a fire in the backyard. Darla had just gotten a new fire pit and my mom thought it would be fun to make s'mores. We could see them arranging logs from the kitchen window.

"Can I ask you a question?" Max said, scrubbing a spaghetti stained plate.

By the serious tone in her voice, I could tell it wasn't going to be a fun conversation. "Sure," I answered.

She concentrated on the plate as she talked. "Do you like Daenan? I mean, it's okay if you do. I mean, I don't care, but I just think he likes you because he's been acting standoffish... it's whatever, I mean—"

"I don't like anyone right now," I said abruptly. "I never really think about that kind of stuff." I thought about when I kissed Daenan and when Max kissed me. "I got other stuff to worry about."

She nodded. "Yeah."

Chapter 9

The next day, Max was standing on Darla's doorstep. She smiled broadly; I could tell she was up to something, "Come with me," she said.

"Where?"

She giggled impishly. "It's a surprise."

I didn't have anything better to do. "How long will I be gone? I need to ask my mom."

Max slouched over and groaned in disgust. Then she stood up straight and said, "Tell her you'll be back before dark."

I popped back into the house to ask. My mom was in the bathroom getting ready for something.

"Mom!" I hollered. "Can I go hang out with Max?"

She came out into the living room. She was wearing a silky champagne dress and black heels, her hair was down and curled, and she was wearing a thick coating of mascara and more lipstick than I'd ever seen her wear (she had probably borrowed the shade from Darla). I was immediately annoyed.

"Are you going somewhere?"

"Oh, I'm just going to meet a friend of Darla's," she said casually.

I narrowed my eyes at her. "Really?"

She ignored me. "Where are you going and when will you be home?"

"We're just gonna hang out at her house," I said, not removing my glare. "I'll be home—" I started, but then quickly changed my mind. "I'm gonna spend the night."

"Okay. Go ahead." She waved a hand, dismissing me.

It was blatantly obvious that my mother was going on a date. I was furious. She wasn't even divorced yet. Just another thing to add to the list of unethical crimes my parents had committed. I could see it now: an unpleasant scene playing out in my head, like the one of my father humping a tattooed girl who couldn't have been more than five years older than me. My mom would be sipping red wine while a sweet nobody whispered things that mothers shouldn't hear into her ear.

"Andy, are you okay?" Max asked, tilting her head to one side as I'd seen her do many times before.

My hands had fallen asleep because I'd been clenching them so long, and the amount of pressure I had applied with my fingers had left red marks on my palms. For once, I was thankful for my nail-biting habit. I uncurled my fingers carefully and stretched them. The tingling was painful.

"Yeah. I'm fine," I replied and motioned with my hand, 'Let's go.' We had reached Max's apartment. "This is the surprise?"

"Nah, silly." She rustled my hair as if I were a child and opened the door. "Just gotta do something first."

The inside of her apartment was not what I'd expected. It smelled of cheap incense and the living room curtains were yellowed. The kitchen table was cluttered with about two week's worth of dishes, unopened mail, and miscellaneous garbage. None of that was surprising. What was surprising was the beautifully painted hand-carved cuckoo clock that hung in the short hallway leading to the bedrooms in the back. I could see all of this from the front door. Max stepped inside, slipped off her high tops and set them beside a pair of work boots.

"Can you take off your shoes please?" she asked. "I just vacuumed."

"Okay?" I said complying to her request, placing my khaki Toms in the line-up of shoes.

Max scurried into the bedroom at the

back of the hallway, then poked her head out to say, "You can come in."

"All right."

When I entered, I was overwhelmed with some sort of plant-like fragrance (I wasn't familiar with flowers and their various smells). I attempted to stifle a cough.

"Oh, sorry," she said as she shook out the incense that had been sitting on the windowsill. "The lady who lived here before us was a smoker." She opened the window "I just hate that smell, you know?"

"Yeah. It's okay."

She had a bunk bed. It was made up with pink sheets, a Pikachu doll was sitting on the pillow, and extra bedding was folded neatly on the top bunk. Her walls were covered in posters of bands I'd never heard of and cutouts of what looked like pictures from Home and Garden magazine. I sat on her bed. It squealed in protest.

"So..." I started as Max dug through her closet, "what's the surprise?"

She whipped her head around. "Duh! It's a surprise," she said, and went back to frantically searching through her closet. "Yes!" she exclaimed in triumph and galloped back into the main room. I followed behind, beginning to wonder what I was getting myself into.

She pushed aside a heap of trash and slammed a plastic tub onto the kitchen table. She tapped her fingernails on the plastic with the same grace as a pianist, but she bounced in her seat like a kid with ADHD. "Do you like crafts?" she asked.

I pursed my lips. "Not really."

"Maxxy!" said a thunderous voice, startling us from behind.

We both turned to look over our shoulders and we saw a man in nothing but sweatpants and the fur that covered his chest. He adjusted his glasses and continued in his overly enthusiastic tone, "I've been here for three nights and this is the first time I've seen you."

"I'm busy," she responded flatly.

"I get it. You got a boyfriend now." He chuckled, squeezing her shoulder and running his fingers through her hair with his other hand. "When did your hair turn blue?"

She shrugged her shoulders away from him. He appeared unfazed. "I'm gonna go get some beer for your pop. I'll be back."

As soon as the door to her apartment shut, she ran into one of the back rooms. I could faintly make out Max saying, "Dad, I'm going to Daenan's. Love you." and a grumble in reply.

"Is there a reason we're going to Daenan's?" I asked as she reentered the room.

"Nah." She left her crafting case on the kitchen table and shoved me out the door. "I'm going to Daenan's. You should go home."

"Who was that?" I asked.

"He's my uncle. Just go, okay?"

Chapter 10

I stood there staring at the big walnut door to my father's study, clutching our favorite book in my hands. I remember being scared, not scared of getting in trouble, but scared of how he would respond; scared to hear his voice again. I was surprised at exactly how high my anxiety level was at the mere thought of seeing my dearly missed father. So I stood there and stared at the door, trying to decide if I wanted to hear his voice.

"Andy sweetie," my mom said from behind me, "what are you doing?"

I turned around to face her, holding out the book for her to see. She obviously knew our tradition. My father had been gone for nearly three and a half months. He had been out of the state working on an important case (that's all my parents told me, anyway). They said I was too young to know what the case was about.

"Daddy's busy right now. You can see him tomorrow. Why don't you come watch a movie with me and Tony downstairs?" Mom said, her voice softening slightly, like she did when she was talking to four-year-old Tony.

I shook my head, stubborn, even at my young age.

She shrugged. "Okay, you can try, but he's busy."

"Daddy?" I said peeking my head into the study. "Will you read me *Huckleberry Finn?*"

He grinned, setting down a pen on an open file folder that was laying on his desk. "Ah, miss Andrea, of course."

My father was a tall, handsome man, with dark hair and chiseled features. He often wore some sort of suit or dress shirt, even at home (that night he was just wearing some khakis and a polo). He was sitting at his desk with his reading glasses perched on the bridge of his nose. I always liked the way he looked when he did that.

I scurried over and he scooted his chair away from the desk so I could hop up onto his lap. He wrapped his arms around me and held the book out in front of me like he always did.

"The Widow Douglas she took me for her son, and allowed she would sivilize

me," he read in a soft voice, *"but it was rough living in the house all the time, considering how dismal regular and decent the Widow was in all her ways; and so when I couldn't stand it no longer I lit it out."*

We read there for almost half an hour before the phone rang.

"Andrea, I gotta take this," he said, laying the opened book down on the desk.

I hopped down from his lap and quickly scooped up the book, not wanting the spine to crease, and wedged a slip of paper between its pages.

"Yes?" he said into the phone and gestured with two fingers for me to go out the door.

I was thinking about this as Tyler and David were wrestling around the living room floor. Tyler's glasses were laying on the coffee table. Tony had put on some cartoons for them to watch, but they showed little interest. Josie was jabbering at them, trying to get involved, but with no luck. She crawled over to where I was sitting on the couch and stood up next to me.

"They won't let me play with them," she whimpered.

"Boys are jerks," I said playfully. All the boys, even Tony, popped their heads up at me as if objecting, but then went back to what they were doing.

"Do you want me to braid your hair?" I asked. "I can make you look like Dorothy."

She beamed, nodding her head rapidly. "Yeah," she said and then paused, "who's Dorothy?"

"Nevermind." I laughed, gesturing to the floor. "Okay. Sit right here."

I started to braid. "So, when are you guys going to your dad's house again?" I asked.

"I don't know."

David shot up out of the tangle of arms and legs; he and Tyler rolled away from each other like a couple of armadillos and sat criss cross on the carpet. Tyler sat there listening while David screamed, "They don't tell us nothing!"

That caught Tony's attention. "They don't tell you who you're staying with?"

David stuck his face out at Tony. "Dad *PISSES* mamma off."

Tyler finally spoke: "Mamma doesn't like us seeing him. We don't see him very much."

He picked his glasses up off the table and put them on; this meant that the roughhousing was over. He picked himself up off of the floor and went to his room.

"Aw! Come on!" David moaned.

Things started to quiet down as David became bored and he succumbed to watching cartoons with Josie.

"Do you miss Dad?" Tony asked in a

hushed tone.

I stood outside my dad's study, giddy with excitement. I shoved the door open. Before I even had a chance to ask, he said, "Yes. Of course, but go get your brother. We wouldn't want him to miss anything."

Tony was six and I was ten. He was finally old enough to start enjoying our favorite book. At first, I was resentful of this new situation, because Tony had taken my spot on Daddy's lap, but I had grown accustomed to it after a couple of chapters. I now had to stand next to him while he wrapped his arms around Tony. Despite my distaste for that, it didn't ruin my love for the story.

He started to read where we had left off the time before, removing the slip of paper from its pages. "*We said there warn't no home like a raft, after all. Other places do seem so cramped up and smothery, but a raft don't. You feel mighty free and easy and comfortable on a raft.*"

I shrugged. "I don't know. I guess."

He hummed thoughtfully. "Well, I do. I bet he's looking for us."

I hoped so, though I wouldn't admit that to Tony. I was beginning to feel the way I did when I was eight years old and he had been gone working on that big case. I missed his voice, but when I tried to remember what it sounded like, I wasn't sure that I wanted to hear it. The memory of the person I loved, my daddy, seemed so far out of reach. I wasn't sure if it was worth the effort to look for it. I didn't reply to Tony's statement; I had no opinion worth sharing. Things were never what they seemed to be when Christian women lied and good men cheated.

The ring of the doorbell broke my train of thought.

"Hey," Daenan said, smiling awkwardly as he stood on Darla's front steps, "I had to get some air and I was wondering if you wanted to come with me."

I couldn't help but laugh. It was about 8:30 p.m. and I had just endured a full day of watching the kids."Yeah, anything to get me out of this house."

"Cool."

It was a short walk, traveling in the opposite direction we would normally take to get to the park. We sat on the brick wall that rimmed the cemetery and talked. Daenan had a bag of Sour Patch Kids that he was snacking on.

"Does it suck being in that house with all those people?" Daenan asked.

I thought for a moment. "Eh, it's not that bad. The kids get on my nerves a lot, but my brother's pretty quiet...Darla's a nurse, so she works a lot, and my mom hasn't been around much since we got here..." I could feel my face tense. "I think she's dating someone."

"Does that piss you off?" he asked.

I shrugged. "It's none of my business."

"That's not what I asked though. Does it piss you off?" he repeated.

"Yeah. I guess."

"You miss your dad?"

I shot him a death glare. Here was another person making assumptions about me again. But Daenan's sense of my feelings wasn't misguided; I did miss him. I sighed and pulled my legs up onto the wall so I could hug my knees and rest my chin on my arms. "When I was little," I started, "my dad used to read *Huckleberry Finn* to me all the time. We must of read it at least a dozen times..." I chuckled, "but you gotta grow up sometime."

We were reading like always. Daddy read, "*I studied a minute, sort of holding my breath, and then I says to myself: 'All right then, I'll go to hell, and tore it up. It was awful thoughts and awful words, but they was said. And I let them stay said; and never thought no more about reforming.*"

He was reading, with Tony on his lap and me at his side, when there was a knock on the door to his study.

"It's time for bed," my mother said.

Tony hurried to his room and I started to head for mine, but she stopped me.

"I think it's time you stop asking Daddy to read you that book," she said flatly.

"Why?" I asked, instantly feeling the tears gathering.

She rolled her eyes. "I think you are too old to be daydreaming over a silly book, let alone being read to at your age."

My mother couldn't begin to comprehend the importance of those meetings with my father and our shared love of that book. I twisted my face up into probably the ugliest pout an eleven-year-old could make. "That's stupid," I protested, crossing my arms.

She looked at me as if I were a bug that needed to be squashed. "You need to focus on more important things…like school, and you're starting soccer practice next week, so you better start conditioning now to get a head start. I'm just going to let your father know that you won't be joining them for the reading from now on. Go get some sleep."

She bent over and tried to kiss me goodnight; I pulled away and marched to my room.

Daenan reached over and put an arm around my shoulders. I jolted a little, surprised, but I leaned into him. I'd never been held by anyone other than my dad. It made me a little anxious, but I warmed up to the moment. It felt peaceful. Then I remembered what it meant…I didn't need anyone. I did not. I pulled away, shoving him away from me and scooting down the wall.

He looked hurt.

After a long pause and attempts at speaking from the both of us, I asked in a soft voice, "Do you ever feel like running? Not going anywhere, just running?"

He shook his head. "No. Not really. I've always sorta wanted to be stable."

I looked at him, asking him to explain with my eyes.

He sighed. "When I was a kid, my parents got arrested for pawning stuff that they stole from our neighbor. Then our neighbor called the cops 'cause he thought they were doing drugs."

I stared at him, probably a little more interested than I should have been. "Were they?"

"Yeah, heroin" he stated as if telling me what he had for breakfast. "Anyway, so I got shipped off from relative to relative. I was living with my grandma for a while, but now I'm living by myself. Got a job and apartment. I *had* a roommate, but he moved."

"Oh."

He hopped down from the wall. "Do you want me to walk you home?"

I shrugged. "Sure."

"My birthday's on Wednesday..." I started, "you can come over if you want."

He gave a small smile. "Yeah. That

would be cool."

We walked awhile in silence. Then I felt Daenan's fingers crawl their way down my wrist and curl around my palm. My heart pounded.

I leapt away from him. "What are you trying to do?" I said with a scowl.

He winced, as if hurt. "Just trying to hold your hand. You don't have to be a bitch about it."

"I'm not being a bitch," I growled, "I just don't need you doing that..."

He snickered. "What are you so afraid of? Do you really think I'm that bad a guy?"

"I'm not afraid of anything!" I shouted. "I don't like you, and I don't need you trying to comfort me. Just because I drunk kissed you and told you something personal, you think I'm in love with you or something? Get over yourself."

He stormed off, muttering, "Wow, okay."

Fuck.

"Wait," I called after him.

He stopped and turned to look at me.

"Listen, I'm perfectly content on my own. I never cared much for my friends at home anyway," I said, attempting an apology. "Don't take it personally."

His eyes softened a bit, but he still kept his distance from me. "So you don't think you need people?"

"Because I don't," I said, unwilling to budge. "Look, I'm sorry. I'll try not to be a such bitch." I gave him a goofy smile. "Will you still walk me home?"

He let out a sigh. "I said I would, didn't I? Come on."

Chapter 11

"So, how did you meet Daenan again?" my mother asked Tony and I, spreading frosting in a cake pan with a spatula.

My birthday... I could not complete the thought, because I couldn't believe we we're actually celebrating it. Before my 13th birthday, I had told my mom that I no longer wanted any parties. I thought they were for children, but something about the move and with everything that had happened, I almost wanted to feel like a kid again. I guess my mom wanted to pretend that she hadn't changed in recent events also...so I went along with it. Now, I was standing in the kitchen making small talk with her while she frosted my birthday cake. It all felt strange. *Today, I'm eighteen.* That's what I kept thinking..

"Andy?" she said in a soft voice.

"Huh? Oh. He's friends with Max. We've hung out a few times," I said finally.

She smiled. "Are you gonna put on that dress Darla got for you. It was really cute."

I shrugged, disappointed that she remembered.

"Andy!" she said in a stern voice, abruptly changing her tone. "Go put it on."

So I went to my room and put on the stupid green dress. *Do I look like an adult in this dress?* I didn't think so. I felt more like a little girl getting ready for an Easter egg hunt. I huffed in frustration and walked briskly back to the kitchen.

There, I walked in on Max awkwardly chatting with my mom. I forced a smile when she looked at me. Her bright eyes matched her perky disposition. "Happy birthday, Andy." She came over close to me and whispered, "Nice dress."

I glared at her defensively. "Shut up."

She laughed. "No, I mean it. You look cute."

She offered a bashful smile, as if she'd said something wrong. Then, she exclaimed, "You look damn sexy!"

We laughed and I took a step away, not wanting to give the wrong impression.

"Where's Daenan?" I asked.

"He's on his way," she beamed. "He wanted to pick up something first."

I smiled. *Daenan got me something?* I wondered what it could be.

The front door opened and there was the sound of children chattering, followed by a desperate Darla calling for help."Can someone help me with this?"

She was carrying Josie, two pizzas, and what looked like a crudely wrapped present. Tyler was tugging at her skirt, and David was blocking her path. Max giggled and took Josie from her, so she could more easily manage the load she was carrying.

Darla, obviously flustered with her children, managed a smile. "Happy birthday, honey. The kids made you something while they were at their dad's."

Daenan appeared in the doorway behind her. He was almost a foot taller than her, despite her being on the steps.

"Hi." I smiled past Darla.

"What?" Darla spun in a circle. "Oh. Come on in honey, and grab a seat."

"Thanks. Where's your bathroom?"

"Oh." Darla pointed to the back of the house. "It's down there on left."

"Okay, thanks."

With that, he disappeared down the hall.

My mom passed out servings of pizza, and as we ate she went around and picked up pop cans and trash that was strewn about.

"What's your birthday wish, Andy?" Max asked.

"Pfft. I don't know," I chuckled.

"And you know the rules," my mom added as she lit the candles on the cake. "If she tells, it won't come true."

A real trip to the mall would be nice. We spent the rest of the night playing Monopoly, which was fun, especially when David got mad and threw the board across the room like a frisbee. The kids had made me one of those macaroni picture frames and I kept wondering what Daenan had gotten me. But nothing had come of it, so I had figured he hadn't gotten me anything. However, when I went to my room after everyone had left, I saw a book sitting on the nightstand between mine and Tony's beds: *The Adventures of Huckleberry Finn.*

I held the book in my hands and thumbed through the pages. It even had that musty old book smell that I loved. As I continued to flip through it, I heard my daddy's voice, repeating our favorite lines: *"It took away all the uncomfortableness and we felt mighty good over it, because it would a been a miserable business to have any unfriendliness on the raft; for what you want, above all things, on a raft, is for everybody to be satisfied, and feel right and kind towards the others."*

In that moment,I missed him more than I'd ever missed him— even more than when he was out of state for almost four months. When I picked up that black-corded phone, that was my only thought as I saw Mom sitting at the dining room table, playing sudoku.

I picked up the phone, trying to think of what I would say to my dad. "Who are you calling?" I heard my mom ask.

I stared at the phone in my hand. "I'm calling dad," I said softly.

The chair clattered as she got up. "No, Andy. It's really late."

She attempted to take the phone from me, but I held it tightly in my hand; the plastic pressed firmly into my fingers.

"I'm calling dad," I repeated.

She released her grip and backed away defeated.

I dialed the number. One ring, two rings—

"Hello?" It was a woman's voice.

My mouth went dry. "Who is this?" I asked.

"Molly. Are you calling for Don?" she asked.

"Yeah..."

"Don, there's a girl on the phone for you," I heard her say slightly muffled as if she didn't want me to hear.

"Hello?" said my dad in his usual chipper voice.

I started to shake. "Dad?"

There was silence on the other end.

Then finally, "It's really late."

"I know, but..." I started, "I wanna

come home. Do you know where I am? I'm sorry mom didn't tell you, but I'm in Reno. You can come get me, or maybe I can fly out there. I just really wanna go home and—"

"Andrea," he cut me off, "I don't know what you're going on about, but your mom should have explained all of this to you. Molly and I are getting married soon. Your mom and I agreed that it would be better if you kids moved in with your mom's cousin for a while. We thought it would make the transition easier."

My head hurt. "What?"

He sighed heavily. "Listen, you're old enough to understand these kinds of things, so I'm not gonna give the speech about how I still love your mom. Your mom and I can't live together anymore and we thought it would be better if you didn't have to go back and forth between houses..."

It all made sense now, only in the most perverted way. "You knew about the move?"

He must not of heard me because he kept talking: "..especially since you're turning eighteen soon. We didn't want it to be more trouble than it needed to be."

"Dad!" I shouted into the phone, shaking with rage...and something else more intense than I'd ever felt before. "I turned eighteen today. My birthday was today."

There was more silence and then: "I'm sorry Andrea, but I have work in the morning."

I hung up the phone. I was shaken.

I headed straight for the door.

"Wait," my mom pleaded and blocked my path.

I shoved past her and left without saying a word.

I started walking, like the night Nicole called me. Only this time, the destination was truly unknown. My legs were the one thing I could count on to carry me. I didn't know where they were taking me, but I didn't care as long as it was away from this house. I didn't want to feel this way anymore, and it wasn't long before I got my wish.

I didn't get far from Darla's house, maybe a few blocks. I think I was close to a 7-Eleven, because I remember seeing green, and white, and red. I saw red.

He grabbed me mid-stride. I didn't see him. I didn't hear him. He squeezed my arm really hard, and, at first I was just really pissed. "Hey!" I screamed at him. "Fuck off!" He tried to tug at my hair, but it was too short for him to get a good grip. I remembered reading that women with long hair were more likely to get attacked, but that didn't help me. What a cruel joke that was. I slapped him, but he still had my arm. He twisted it around, causing immediate pain. Then, with the hand he used to pull my hair, he pinched the back of my neck as if I were some sort of animal that needed to be subdued. I kicked and punched at him, but my defensive attempts failed as he got a hold of me from behind.

He drug me somewhere away from the streetlights, but it felt like I wasn't far from the street. All I could do was thrash wildly to try to break free and get a glimpse of his face. Finally, he let go of my arm for a moment, but seconds later I was on the pavement with a severe pain shooting across my back.

A moment later, he was climbing on top of me, but I summoned enough strength in my legs to push him off, just long enough to see his eyes. They were a familiar dark color and framed by a pair of wire-rimmed glasses that I remembered seeing somewhere before. Before he could make another move, I gave him my best kick, which knocked him back a few steps. But just as I thought I may be able to run, I saw his knife, the blade glimmering in the moonlight.

He grabbed me with both hands, and with one swift motion, flipped me over onto my stomach as if I were piece of meat. He reached up my skirt and pressed one hand against my thigh, right under my ass, and held me down. I struggled to pull myself up on my elbows and right as I was going to stand, I felt a sharp pain in the back of my right calf.

My voice cracked as my scream echoed through the alley. The pain was incredibly intense, but it was nothing compared to when he slashed my other leg. The physical agony was nearly unbearable, but the emotional trauma was worse. All I could do is cry. *How could someone do this to another human being?* He was taking my body, the only thing that was truly mine. Now, my body was broken. It was torn.

I passed out. I don't know for how long. When I woke up, I could hear grunting and panting. I could feel his sweat dripping down my face, and I could smell the beer on his breath. And I cried. I cried because I was lying there. I cried because I wasn't in control. I cried because I knew those eyes. He was waiting for me and I didn't see him coming. Nothing in the world was mine. He took the only thing I really had.

When it was over, he left me there. I couldn't move. I couldn't get up off the pavement. All I could do was weep and pray for help.

I wasn't sure how long I laid there, but it was long enough that I thought about death. But just as things were at their darkest, there was hope in the form of footsteps nearby. Of course, there was a part of me that thought it may be the attacker returning, but I had to imagine it was someone else, someone to save me.

I craned my neck in the direction of

the footsteps. Standing above was a man with a grey beard and tattered jeans. He looked down at me, examining me carefully. "Are you hurt, miss?"

I looked down at my pretty green dress, now dyed red, and replied in a coarse voice, "Yes."

He looked at me for a moment longer and then walked briskly out of sight.

Chapter 12

When I woke up, I felt strange. I gripped at a fuzzy material, which startled me. I normally slept with cotton blankets, never fleece. I opened my eyes to harsh florescent lights. After my eyes adjusted, it became clear that I was in a hospital, but I couldn't remember why.

I hopped down from the bed and felt cold like I was naked, but as I looked down at my body, I realized that I was wearing a hospital gown. I continued to examine my surroundings. There were four beds in the room, including my own. Two of the other three were empty and the remaining bed was occupied by a sleeping woman wired up to all sorts of machines. There were no hospital staff members in sight, so I made my way out into the hallway.

I didn't get very far before I was stopped by a young man in magenta scrubs. Judging by the way he was gawking at me, I imagined I didn't look so great.

"Uh... uh, miss," he stuttered, "I'll get a doctor. Uh, wait here please. Please, don't move."

His behavior made me nervous. "Why?" I asked.

His face started to turn pale. "You're uh...bleeding. Just uh...stay there please."

He ran off. I examined the front of my body, inching down it with my eyes, and there was no sign of blood until I reached my feet. I was standing in a puddle, with blood coming up between my toes. There were no visible cuts on my feet. I wondered where the blood was coming from. Then it occurred to me that if I had produced that much blood where I was standing, I must have left a trail. I turned to look behind me and sure enough, there was the trail of blood leading from my room. I looked down again and pivoted one of my legs so that I could see the back of it. There was a steady stream of blood flowing down the back of my calf. That's when it hurt.

The pain was followed by an immediate realization of why I was in the hospital. I had been raped.

I screamed, bellowing cries that echoed through the hall, but I didn't feel the release that came from crying.

I just kept crying. Then I remembered what my father had told me. He didn't want me home. I was so upset and I just wanted to walk.Why wasn't I allowed to walk?

Feelings of helplessness and sadness quickly turned to anger. How could he do this? He had no right to take what he did from me; yet here I was, screaming, covered in tears and in blood. In this moment, I thought of my father. I needed his support, his embrace. He was the only man whom I loved.

The young man returned with a woman and I was lifted into a wheelchair. I was carted off to another room where I was forced to lie face down on a metal table. The woman spoke softly, "You tore your stitches, we're gonna have to restitch your legs."

I got out a small, "Okay," through the sobs.

"Would you like to hold Dylan's hand?" she said, pointing at the young man wearing the magenta scrubs. "He's a nice boy."

I took a deep breath and held out my hand, which was probably sweaty. I was still sobbing and I found it hard to breathe. I could feel the snot collecting on my upper lip, and my chest was wet with tears. I had not bothered to wipe them away, so they had run all over, soaking through my hospital gown.

The woman walked behind me and out

of sight. I felt something cold against my leg. Then, it stung, and I squeezed Dylan's hand. He winced. After she was done cleaning up my legs, I felt a slight pulling sensation trace down my calves. Luckily, it didn't last long.

"Is that it?" I asked, blinking through some of the mist in my eyes.

"Not yet sweetheart," she replied, "but soon."

I felt a poke in my left leg and then it went numb. I let go of Dylan's hand. The tugging lasted a while longer that time, but it didn't hurt. When she was done, they lifted me up off the table and put me down in the wheelchair.

The woman looked down at a clipboard that was sitting on a counter to the right of me. Her eyebrows knitted together and she stared at it intensely for a moment.

She cleared her throat. "Andrea," she said, meeting my eyes, "is there anyone we can call for you? Maybe your mom?"

I shook my head vigorously. "No. Don't call my mom. Please don't call my mom," I pleaded, my heart beating faster.

I couldn't take seeing my mom's reaction to what had happened. I didn't want to see her cry. The nurse put up a hand. "It's okay, we won't call her if you don't want us to. Is there anyone else you would like us to call."

I didn't want to go back to Darla's and I couldn't go to Max's, because her dad was there, or even worse, my attacker might have been there.

"Can you call my friend, Daenan?" I requested. She handed me the clipboard so I could write his number down. As I did this, she explained, "We are going to discuss some sensitive topics. It's good if you have someone here with you."

I nodded.

Daenan arrived shortly. "What happened?" he demanded, almost yelling. The woman took his arm and led him outside. A few minutes later, he stormed back in. His face was red with anger. "I'm gonna kill him."

"Daenan," I said softly, "don't."

His nostrils were flaring. He rubbed his hands over his face, making swift movements, and his chest heaving. He came over to me and sat down in the chair beside mine. He took my hand and started rubbing it between his. I let him hold my hand.

"We would like you to do a rape kit," the woman stated. "Would you be willing to do that?"

I stopped crying right then. I looked her in the eyes. In that moment, all I could think of was Max. It all made sense now. Considering the way she acted at the park and at her apartment, he must have been her uncle. He would hurt her. Again. And again. And I had the ability to stop it. "I'll do it," I said.

After the procedure, some nurses gave me a sponge bath so I didn't get my legs wet and I asked Daenan to get me a change of clothes from my house. Daenan left for about an hour. When he returned he had my sport bag from my closet with a couple pairs of sweatpants, several t-shirts, some underwear and my toothbrush. After I was dressed and clean, they returned me to my wheelchair and put me by a window. Someone brought me tea. I wasn't sure who, because I was so tired. Everything was like white noise to me. Daenan looked tired too. He sat next to me, resting his cheek on his palm. "How did I get here?"

Daenan lifted his head. "Huh?"

"To the hospital, I mean."

"Oh, uh, I think the nurse said some homeless guy found you. He must have went and got somebody."

"Oh." My thoughts were empty for a while and we didn't speak. But then I remembered Daenan's trip to Darla's house. "Did you see my mom when you went to Darla's?"

He shook his head. "Tony let me in. He asked if you were okay."

I imagined that my brother must have known about me calling our dad. "What did you say?"

"I just told him you were upset."

"Oh."

There was another long pause. Then finally I said, "I wanna see him."

"Tony?"

"No, the man who found me."

At my request, Daenan rolled me to the front desk. I had to arch my neck to see over the top of the counter. An old man sat at a computer with his back to me.

"Excuse me," I said, getting his attention.

He looked down at me. "Oh, you must be Andrea. How can I help you?" I cringed. It occurred to me that he must have detailed information about me at his desk somewhere.

"Who brought me in here?" I asked, chewing at my lip.

"Oh, just George." he said with a smile and pointed at a disheveled looking man asleep in the lobby. "I think he's been waiting to see you."

I nodded. "Thank you." And Daenan wheeled me over to him.

"George?"

He snorted, waking from what seemed to be a deep sleep. "Yes, uh, what'r you waking me up for?" he said, slurring his words. His eyes widened when he saw me. "Oh you're, uh, I'm sorry, ma'am."

"No. It's ok."

Daenan put a hand on my shoulder.

"I just wanted to thank you for your help. I might have died if someone hadn't found me in time."

He looked me up and down. "No, ma'am. I just saw you were hurt. You don't have to thank me. I'm glad you're all fixed up now."

"Mostly." I chuckled looking down at my legs. "Anyway, I just wanted to say thank you. I'm gonna go back to my room now."

Chapter 13

The next day, Daenan took me back to his apartment. I still couldn't do much walking. The doctor had said that only the laceration in my left calf was a real problem, and since it had penetrated into the muscle tissue, mobility was obviously a challenge. Luckily, as I was told, the wound on my other leg might not even leave a scar.

And things would have been much worse without someone to literally lean on for support. As I recovered, Daenan helped me a lot. When we got to his apartment, he set me down in the living room and quickly went around picking up beer cans and other varieties of trash spread evenly on all surfaces. After a few minutes, he came and sat down beside me. "Do you wanna watch a movie or something?"

I shrugged. "You don't have to keep a constant eye on me you know?"

"I know." He looked at me with the same sad expression he'd been wearing since he'd arrived at the hospital, which annoyed me, but I tried to be as gentle as possible. "I'm okay. I'm fine. Really." It was funny how I ended up being the one to take care of him in a way.

He just stared at me.

"Can I borrow your phone?" I asked. "I want to call my mom and let her know I'm okay."

He pulled his phone out of his pocket and handed it to me.

The phone only rang once. "Hello?" said my mom's voice.

"Mom—" I started.

"Andy? Where have you been? You can't just disappear for three days without telling me where you are. You're lucky Tony told me you were at Daenan's. I almost called the police. You are gonna have to—"

"Mom!" I yelled, not really caring about the consequences. "Shut up. God!"

"Excuse me," she started up again, "what makes you think you can talk to me that way? Just because you're eighteen now, you think you don't have to show me respect anymore? Is that it?"

The lecture was too much. I didn't have the patience and it was already giving me a headache. "No, mom."

"What then?"

"You suck okay? You lied to me and Tony. And if that wasn't enough, you started dating again without telling me anything about a divorce or any of that shit. So excuse me if I'm a little pissed at you right now."

There was a long silence on the other end. For a second, I thought we had disconnected, but then I heard, "I'm sorry. Andy...being a mom is hard. What am I supposed to say?"

I sighed loudly. "I'm gonna be staying here for a while. I don't know how long. Just thought you should know I'm fine. Bye." I hung up before she had a chance to respond.

The phone rang immediately after, but I didn't pick it up.

"Do you have any books?" I asked Daenan, changing the subject.

"Not really," he replied, "I don't really read."

I sighed. "It's okay. Let's just watch a movie."

I dozed off at some point during the movie (I don't remember what it was called, something with "potatoes" in the title). As I slept, I dreamt of black. No, not black. It wasn't even dark really, it just wasn't light. I felt bodiless, but confined, like I was air that was being compressed. Then I felt an unpleasant cold, more like being wet. I was then aware that my actual body was in discomfort. I was sweaty and was struggling to breathe. I wriggled in my sleep, trying to break free from that feeling. My head felt heavy. Then I felt heavy, and I felt as if I were drowning. I gasped for air.

Then I woke up.

"Andy, it's okay." Daenan's arms wrapped around me tightly. My head was resting against his chest and he was cradling me as if I were a small child. I hadn't noticed that I had been moved from the position I'd fallen asleep in. He started stroking my hair. My chest heaved up and down as I caught my breath. I didn't speak.

"You were whining. I thought you were having a nightmare or something."

He waited for me to respond, but I didn't have the energy to. I just laid there.

He stopped stroking my hair. "Sorry," he said and gently lifted me off of him so I was sitting up. He got up from the couch and I watched him disappear into the kitchen. He returned a moment later with a beer. He opened it and handed it to me. "Here."

I went to take a sip, but as I smelled its pungent odor, my stomach lurched in rejection. I remembered the last time I had smelled beer...*that man's breath on my face.* I attempted to head for the bathroom, but vomited as soon as I stood. It splashed across the carpet. I felt disgusting.

Daenan took a step towards me.

"Don't," I said, thrusting a hand in his direction. I wiped my mouth and stood there for what felt like an eternity, my legs shaking beneath me.

Then I stepped, still trembling, around the puddle on the floor and went to brush my teeth. Afterwards, I went into Daenan's room and laid on his bed, staring into the dark, feeling completely useless. I was a coward; I still hadn't told anyone what had happened and I'd had Daenan waiting on me hand and foot since he'd come to be with me at the hospital.

"I'm really sorry." I heard his voice behind me, but I didn't turn around to look at him. "What can I do?"

I thought for a moment. Then sat up, rubbing my fingers through my sweat soiled hair. "I'll be better tomorrow," I promised. "Then, I want to see Max...I want to talk to her."

"Okay," he agreed and then slid into bed next to me.

A few days passed and Max came over unannounced. It was the first time I'd seen her since my birthday party.

"I knew you guys had something going on. You coulda told me, you know?" she declared triumphantly as she danced around Daenan's apartment, which had my belongings strewn about, making it quite obvious I'd been staying there.

I couldn't help feeling a little lighter just seeing her.

"So..." she drew out the word expectantly, "what are we doing here just sitting around." She skipped over to me and tugged at my arms. "There's another rave tomorrow night. We got a shit ton of—woah, what's up with your legs?"

"Has your uncle been around lately?" I asked, ignoring her question.

Her smile melted from her face. "No..." she said, rubbing her arm. "Why?"

Suddenly, I didn't feel light anymore. I sighed, gulping down my anxiety. "He...I was walking and he..."

I couldn't say it out loud. I looked at Daenan; I looked at him to save me from the words. *Please.*

"She was raped," he said; such ugly words.

She was quiet, and she went stiff. Her eyes were foggy. She plopped down beside me.

"Why don't you say something?" I asked.

She didn't respond and refused to look at me.

"Why?" I said, my face getting hot. "Nothing to say?"

"Andy, stop," said Daenan softly.

"No! I can't stop. What the fuck are we doing here? Seriously."

I should've noticed that Max was crying, but I didn't. I was shaking too much. My head was pulsing. My stomach lurched. Churning. Aching. My whole body was burning up.

"It's all so depressing isn't it? Of course it is? Right." I wasn't sure when I started screaming. "I'm some broken shell of a person now, right? You both feel so sorry for me, right? You relate to me? I'm angry! I'm fucking angry. I'm just...fucking angry...all right?"

My chest heaved as I tried to catch my breath and Max briskly headed for the door. It thudded against the wall when it swung open.

"You're just leaving?" I asked.

She turned back to face me, mascara running down her cheeks. "I hate him."

Before I could think of whether or not to make her stay, she was gone.

Chapter 14

A few more days passed, and I had been asked to go to the police station for a follow-up interview regarding my initial statement about my assault. I was sitting across from Detective Berkley.

I looked him up and down as he sat on top of a shiny metal table. His hands rested on his knees and he was speaking to me in a warm voice, although I wasn't sure what he was saying anymore because something about him made me think about my dad. Despite his coffee colored skin, curly hair, and the fact that he was probably at least sixty, his attire—a tightly tucked salmon-colored shirt, medium wash blue jeans and a pair of old red and white Nikes—oddly struck me. I couldn't help but compare him to my father. The only time my dad would ever wear jeans was when we were camping or when he took Tony and I fishing. Plus, he would never have let his shoes get so dirty, and seeing that bright salmon colored shirt almost made me laugh, because all I knew my dad would never have worn that color...except maybe now...maybe now that he was marrying that young girl. I hated them both.

That's not to say that my parents belonged together; they probably didn't. In fact, their personalities didn't seem to jibe with each other at all. My mother was rigid, superstitious, and she could be cold whereas my father was intelligent, charismatic, but also compassionate. So, in looking back, I started to wonder if their entire relationship was a facade. I found myself recalling our every conversation and playing them back in my head, trying to find the falsehoods.

A hand waved in my face. "Andrea, are you ready to continue?"

I looked up at the smiling Detective Berkley, blinking my eyes, feeling as if he had suddenly appeared before me. I had never had this much trouble concentrating in my life. I was very tired. I'd felt tired ever since I'd woken up in the hospital. "Yeah," I replied, still barely lucid.

He looked at me with kind eyes. He was obviously a very patient man. "I was just saying that, with your hospital records from the night of the attack, and assuming that George Parr is willing to give his eyewitness testimony, we should be able to convict him. You might not even need to testify."

"That's good," I said, once again distracted by his shirt.

He dropped his head, making more direct eye contact with me. "You can go. I think that's all we need for now Andrea, I will give you a call if I think of anything else. I'm gonna do everything I can to put this monster behind bars."

"Okay." I got up from my chair.

"Can I offer you a ride home? You do have a place to stay, don't you?" the detective asked.

"Yes, I have a..." I said with pause when thinking about how exactly to classify Daenan at this point, "...a friend coming to pick me up."

Later, I found myself back at Daenan's apartment, but I wasn't sure if he had indeed picked me up from the station, or if I had walked. I staggered through the front door, in somewhat of a trance. It almost felt like I was sleepwalking. The thoughts that passed through my mind were coherent, but devoid of emotion. *Where is Daenan?* I was overwhelmed by a strange disorientation, like the world was being tipped to the left and gravity was pulling me downward. I hugged the wall for balance and sank to the floor, staring at a tuft of carpet that was longer than the rest.

I wasn't sure how much time had passed before I finally lifted myself off the floor. I may have been dehydrated, emotionally wiped or just physically exhausted, but it was all the more likely I was a little of each.

I stumbled into into the kitchen like a zombie. There was a large knife laying on the counter. It must have been the knife Daenan had used when cooking dinner the night before. I stared at it for a long time and I had the strangest desire. I just wanted to run it over my skin. I just wanted to feel the cool blade and even test its sharp edge. But of course, I knew what would happen if I did that. I knew it would hurt and that I would bleed. Even still, I couldn't help but stare at the knife and think of these things. I imagined taking the knife and running it across my neck, and the blood running down.

I jolted back at the thought and hurried out of the kitchen, pacing back and forth in the living room. I pulled at my hair and hit the top of my head with my fist. "Stop it. Stop it. Stop it," I said to myself. No matter how hard I tried, I couldn't get out of the fog I was in. Then I felt tears rolling down my cheeks. *Why was I crying?* I ran into Daenan's room and shut the door. I sat on his bed and I waited. I couldn't hurt myself if I just sat there.

Similar violent thoughts stayed with me for two more nights, but instead of engaging with them in some way, I'd simply disconnect, attempting to unplug my mind from everything that I was feeling. Daenan tried hard to help me remain present, but all I could think about was my father and how he had disregarded me, as if I were someone he barely knew. I just let myself sink deeper and deeper into this pit of self-loathing. *How could I love someone so much that didn't love me? He couldn't possibly reciprocate that love, could he? No. And what about Tony? If he loved us, he wouldn't have let us leave. If he loved us, he wouldn't of sounded so cold when I called him. If he loved us, he would have called me.*

"Andy," Daenan pleaded. "Andy, are you okay?" he asked even though he knew I wasn't. He ran his fingers between my shoulder blades and whispered, "Andy, talk to me. You can talk to me." He hugged me tightly. It didn't feel special, like it's supposed to feel when someone holds you. I was stiff. Then I heard a sniffle. I looked, and saw that tears were collecting in his eyes. Daenan wasn't the type to cry. That's all it took. I was awake.

"Stop, stop." I wiped a tear from his cheek. "Don't cry. I'm fine."

"Stop pulling that shit!" he screamed as his face turned a sort of bruised color for a moment. Then, he hugged me tighter than before. I caressed the nape of his neck, feeling the short prickly hairs under my fingers.

It had been two weeks since I'd left the hospital and Max seemed determined to put things back to normal. She spun on her heels, with a big rainbow colored bag over her shoulder and her arms crossed over her chest. She scowled. "Fucking hell! You guys are worse than a couple of retired ladies who just had their favorite soap opera canceled." Her smile spread from ear to ear, but with a more sinister vibe than usual. She tapped her fingernails across a transparent plastic case that was sitting on the coffee table. There were some sort of brightly colored objects inside. I recognized them from my time at her apartment. "There's gonna be a rave downtown tonight and I haven't been to one in a long ass time, so we're going."

Daenan pulled his phone from his pocket. It vibrated in his hand. "Hello?"

He listened for a moment and then handed it to me. It was Detective Berkley. "Hello, Andrea. I wanted to let you know that a warrant has been issued for the arrest of Harvey Anderson. We haven't located him yet. Stay safe, and we'll let you know when we track him down."

"Okay...I will." I hung up the phone.

I cleared my throat, looking at Max. "They're trying to arrest your uncle, but they can't find him."

She stared at me blankly for a moment, shook her head and declared that she didn't "give a fuck". Disregarding the information I'd just given her, she pounded her palms on top of the plastic case, as if beating a drum.

"I made these for you guys. Come on! Look," she insisted.She groaned loudly, threw open the case and pulled out a small bundle of bracelets in various colors that were made out of the same kind of plastic beads that I had seen in her apartment. I vaguely recalled seeing Max wearing a bracelet like that once before.

"Candy?" Daenan cocked his head in disgust.

I thought of the candy beads Tony and I used to get when we were little.

"What?" Max giggled, "No, K-A-N-D-I. You give them to people. Aren't they cute? It took me all last night to make these." She put her hands on her hips, beaming with pride.

"I don't know..." I started, "my legs haven't completely healed yet. I don't want people to see my stitches."

"Worst excuse ever!" she screeched. "Good thing I brought you these."

She reached into her massive bag and pulled out a pair of horrendously brightly colored Galaxy leggings. "Now, you won't stand out."

Daenan rolled his eyes.

"Come on," she whined, "dressing up is

half the fun."

The lighting was dim, with flashes of red, pink, yellow, purple, and green. Some sort of dance music was playing at a deafening volume. Max took me by the wrist and drug me along as she shoved her way through the sea of people, and Daenan trailed close behind. The thumping bass was so heavy that it shook the dance floor. It was hot and the room smelled of sweat, but that didn't detract from the fun I was having.

Max's petite body moved fluidly and effortlessly, as her hips swayed from side to side. Her shirt inched its way off of her shoulders as she moved, revealing her pale flesh underneath. She put a hand on my ribcage, which crept to my back. She ran her finger over my spine, sending a tingling sensation through every inch of my body. Daenan stood passively, swaying a couple feet away.

Their faces flashed blue and yellow under the lights. A fog began to collect in the room, creating a dream-like atmosphere. Out of the corner of my eye, I spotted a young man in a fuzzy pink spirit hood and green shirt, with Kandi covering his arms from wrist to elbow. His was wearing some sort of surgical mask that had been doodled on with rainbow sharpies. His eyes locked with mine as I danced with Max. Daenan puffed out his chest, looking like a bull about to charge. I gave him a stern look and looked back to Max who mouthed the word "go." The boy with the mask still stared at me intensely, as if attempting to summon me. I started to walk in his direction. He nodded and disappeared into the crowd.

I searched for him, checking faces as I moved in the same direction he had. A pair of hands fell down on my shoulders. I jumped and spun around, prepared for anything. It was the boy. He pointed at me, his body convulsing in place as if he were laughing hysterically, despite him being inaudible. Without warning, he put both hands on my hips and yanked me toward him, forcing his body into mine. I still couldn't see his face, but his eyes seemed to rip a hole into me. He rubbed his body against mine, keeping me confined in a small space.

I suddenly couldn't breathe. I wanted to get away from him, but when I tried to move he held me there. I shoved at his chest and I tried to scream, but couldn't hear myself over the music. So, I punched him hard in the gut, causing him to wince in pain. I turned quickly to look for Daenan, and started to cut my way through the crowd. That's when I felt a sharp pain in my side, like something had bitten me.

I whipped around and there he was, the masked kid, who was now hurrying to get away from me. I started to go after him, but I stepped on something, slipped, and my knees hit the concrete floor hard. It was a syringe. I rolled it between my fingers. *The kid fucking stabbed me with a needle. Gross.* I knew I had to get it looked at right away (who knew what the sicko had shot me up with). But first, I had to find Max and Daenan. I pulled myself off the ground and did my best to get through the crowd, but then I started to get dizzy.

The lights seemed to get brighter as my vision only became hazier. The people were starting to melt into the colors of the lights, and the lights seemed to melt into the music. I felt like I was under water. *What am I doing? Where am I going again? Right, I remember...Daenan...and find Max.* I stumbled my way around, guarding my body with my arms clutched around my stomach, while making the tightest fists I could. Out of my peripheral vision, I caught a glimpse of a face that stuck out from among the others. Who was that? I tried to shake the face from my mind and focus on the task at hand. *Just find Daenan and Max.*

But then, I saw a flash of something else: the salt and pepper hair, the wire-rimmed glasses. *No. It couldn't be... but it was. Max's uncle.* Everything was spinning and suddenly, he was gone. I had a massive headache. *Just find them. Just find them. Just find them.* I held my head. It was throbbing. Colors were flashing, blending in with the faces and the fog, and it was all so confusing. *Come on Andy. You can do this. Just find them.* I felt like I was swinging from a playground tire.

I saw him again. He smiled at me the way he had smiled at Max when we were at her apartment. He stood casually with his hands in his pockets. *Not now. Not now. Not now.* My heart swelled inside my chest. *Maybe I'm imagining he's here. But what if he is here? Fuck. I need to find them. I need to get out of here.* I wheezed, struggling to breathe, unsure if the stress of seeing him again was causing me to hyperventilate or if it had something to do with whatever I had been injected with. I stumbled into the person next to me. They stuck out their tongue in disgust and shoved me to the side. I need to find them. *I need to hurry. What if he gets me?* I started to gag.

Purple, green, pink, orange, red, blue, yellow...face after face after face. *I'm never going to find them.* Purple, green, pink...orange...red...blue...*blue. Fucking blue. Max.* Her hair shimmered in the light. I grabbed at her, never so relieved in my life, and refused to let go.

It wasn't long before we got back to the entrance. I had no idea how much time had passed and I didn't care. She leaned me up against the brick wall outside and then pulled a...phone out of her pocket and fiddled with it, tapping her foot on the pavement, a dark expression on her face.

"Your uncle," I said. "I saw him..." I dropped my head due to the dizziness, but quickly brought my focus back to Max, her sapphire eyes wide with what I assumed was fear.

"Someone stuck me with something..." I said in my failed attempt to explain that it could have been a hallucination, but my thoughts weren't translating well into speech.

The doors to the club swung open with a loud clang, as Daenan crashed through the doorway. "What happened?"

"She said someone stuck her with something. I think she's having a bad trip."

"I saw him," I repeated. Then I felt water on my cheeks. Either it was rain or I was crying. I couldn't tell.

"I need to go...to the doctor..." I attempted to stand up. My legs were shaky. Max supported me.

"I'll call a taxi," Daenan said.

Chapter 16

"The doctor said you just need to wait it out," Daenan informed me, even though I'd heard it three times already. He handed me a juice pouch.

"Okay, buddy," Max commanded, shoving Daenan towards his room, "I got this. You have work tomorrow."

Daenan looked back at me, opening his mouth as if to say something, but apparently changed his mind and headed off to bed.

"Why?" I asked, still not totally present in reality. I stared at her, my mouth hanging open, but I was too out of it to care.

She chuckled silently. "'Cause, he's been babysitting for like ever. I can play mommy for a while."

I was not comprehending everything she was saying. The only response I could muster was, "Uh..."

She let out a sigh. "He told me about the little episodes, or whatever, that you've been having the last few nights... it's totally cool though. I get it."

"So, it's not about the drugs?"

She took a seat on the coffee table in front of me. "Nope."

I sprawled out across the couch. I sat there silently, letting that thought brew in my head and the more sober I got, the more it pissed me off. Max didn't even try to make conversion, she just got up and left. A moment later she returned with her oversized bag and pulled out a bottle of neon green nail polish. Then she sat criss-cross on the floor painting her nails.

"Why do I need babysitting anyway?" I asked abruptly, my face tight with irritation. I sat back up, crossing my arms.

Max ignored my question, putting her hand out in front of her to admire the artistry.

"What's your favorite color?" she inquired.

"What?" It seemed like such a meaningless question. I thought we'd been past that point in our friendship.

"What's your favorite color?" she repeated, still looking down at her freshly polished nails.

"Why?"

"Just answer," she insisted, finally looking up at me.

I scoffed. "Orange, I guess."

She hummed in thought, eyeing her nails once more. "I never see you wear a lot of color...so I was just wondering. I bet you could guess my favorite color." She flashed a devilish smile, her eyes sparkling that deep sapphire.

I rolled my eyes. "Blue?"

"Ha!" She leapt from the floor triumphantly and shot a finger in my direction. "You're wrong!"

I sat up in my seat, glaring at her, both perplexed and irked by her making small talk. Her smile was blinding.

"You think I'm blue, but I'm not. You're blue!" she shouted like a deranged five-year-old.

"What the fuck are you talking about?"

She plopped down on the couch beside me. "I love you, Andy." She put an arm around my shoulder. "Quit letting what happened fuck with your head."

I squirmed underneath her arm. "You just don't get it."

"What don't I get?" she said, recoiling from me. She must have been offended, understandably, I admit. But it was more than just that.

I felt the words in the back of my throat, but they seemed to be lodged in my windpipe. I had no idea how to get out what had been eating away at me since that night. It all began to replay in my head. *"You're old enough to understand these kinds of things,"* I heard my dad say in the same voice that always melted my heart and made me feel so safe when I was a kid. I started to shake. I missed him more than I could stand. *"We thought it would be better if you didn't have to go back and forth between houses."* The excuses. *"I'm not gonna give the speech about how I still love your mom."* The indifference toward my mom. *"Especially since you're turning eighteen soon."* Forgetting my birthday. And the worst thing he said was seemingly innocuous. He didn't even have to try to be cruel. *"I'm sorry Andrea, but I have work tomorrow."* He dismissed me. Like I was nothing to him. Why?

My throat tightened, trying to keep down the one truth that I'd been desperately trying to ignore. My nose began to run and I knew within seconds, I'd be a mess of snot and tears. I could've just ignored it. Maybe it would have just gone away. But I couldn't have. My throat hurt too much. I would surely choke on my own denial.

"He doesn't want me home," I let out in a small whisper.

"What?" Max said.

"My dad..."

It wasn't true. It couldn't be true...but it was.

"...doesn't want me to come home. He doesn't want me."

I barely got the words out, and as soon as they were, I was a mess just like

I had predicted.

"Aw shit," she muttered, "I'm sorry, Andy."

There was a long silence. Long silences were something I'd gotten used to over the summer. There's a quiet comfort you feel when everyone has run out of apologies, and excuses, and wise words. The lies stop too. Lies of, "Everything will be okay," are too hollow to speak, and won't be spoken. Silence is a void. And that void is filled with understanding. Max understood that she couldn't make things go back to the way they were and she didn't try.

"I'm a bad person," she said.

I knew what she was going to say next, so I didn't ask.

"I'm sorry I made you go with me tonight. I'm crazy, you know? I hated you when you told me about him."

I shivered. What she said didn't hurt. It made sense to me, as odd as that was.

"I can't think about him, you know? And it's my fault..." her voice trailed off.

"What's your fault?"

"He wouldn't have hurt you if you hadn't met me...and Daenan..." She got up from the couch and stood in front of me, her eyes on the floor, with a dark shadow cast over her face.

"Max...did he..." I said, standing to approach her. As I did, she stepped simultaneously backward. "No," she said. Her tears fell like a light rain. I had a feeling that "no" wasn't an answer to my question. She shook.

"Max..." I tried to be with her as Daenan had been with me.

When she spoke, I could barely hear her. "I'm ashamed," she said.

I wrapped my arms around her. I felt her pain, more than I wanted to. I wiped her tears and when I kissed her, I could taste the salt on her lips. It felt more real than the first time we kissed. It felt more real than anything really. Max was everything beautiful about women and everything forbidden about them at the same time. And what should've happened next? I suppose we should've fallen in love and that we should've run off with each other and eloped. Rode off into the desert or some shit like that. But what if that wasn't what I wanted? What if I just wanted to feel what I felt and never wanted to say it. All I wanted to do was sleep and that's what I told her. I chose sleep—for the time being.

Blood. There'd been a lot of blood ever since that night—my blood. But for the first time, it was his blood. I never expected to see his blood. Though I shouldn't have been surprised; I knew deep down that Daenan had been hurting, and it would've only been a matter of time before he'd do something to take out his anger.

It was really early in the morning and he had been gone the whole day before. I couldn't sleep, so I was awake when he got back. When he came in the front door he was barefoot. His face was bloodied and bruised, his knuckles too. He'd broken his nose, but he didn't seem to care. "I quit my job," was all he said when he came in. He didn't explain the blood, or the bruises, or his lack of footwear.

Max had already gone home, so it was just the two of us. I had him go sit in the bathroom and I went to the kitchen to get some ice for his bruises. He let me clean him up, but he seemed to stare right through me. "What happened?" I asked.

"Nothing," he said still not making eye contact.

I held up his bruised hand and waved it at him. "This isn't nothing."

He pulled away. "I just got in a fight at work."

The expression on his face told me he wasn't going to explain any of it.

I ran a hand through his hair. He looked like shit. He was quiet, his eyes were hollow and red, as though he'd been crying. He almost seemed ill. He leaned into me, resting his head on my stomach. I could feel his hair through my shirt. Everyone was tired, it seemed.

He sat up straight again, sighed, and I kissed his forehead.

He looked up at me, finally making eye contact. "I want to be alone."

"Are you sure?"

"Yeah. Just go home, Andy." He said. "Please."

"Are you sure?" I asked again, not wanting to leave him the way he was.

"Yes." He said, forcing a smile. " Go home. See your mom. I'll be fine."

He was right. It was time for me to go home.

I stood in front of the screen door. My confidence had faded, and I felt like a little girl again—the same one who waited outside her daddy's study, clutching onto her favorite book, terrified to ask to be read to after missing him during his three-month-long business trip. I quietly opened the screen door and let myself into Darla's home.

The house was still asleep and the air was heavy. It was 8:27 a.m., which meant that I had three minutes before my mom would be up for her morning coffee.

I crept my way through the tiny house and into the back bedroom, where my brother was snoring peacefully in his twin-sized bed. I pulled my suitcase from the closet, unzipped the front pocket, and retrieved the letter from the University of Denver. I tucked it into my pocket, went to the kitchen, sat at the kitchen table and waited. My mother meandered into the kitchen wearing her robe and slippers, too groggy to notice me at first. She blinked at me in disbelief, then shouted, "Andy?"

A loud thud came from the back of the house, followed by the pounding of footsteps. Tony slid across the linoleum on his socks, almost colliding with the kitchen counter. "Andy's back?"

"Yeah, doofus" I shot back at him.

"Have you eaten? I'll make you breakfast," Mom said. Pancakes?"

I nodded. "Pancakes."

My mom continued to put pancakes on my plate until I felt nauseous. She didn't speak, she just cooked while Tony gleefully showed me his newest treasure. "Darla got me a sketchbook." He flipped through the pages with pride, showing off sketches of comic book characters and mythical creatures. Suddenly, he stopped and pressed the book against his chest. "Promise you won't make fun of me."

"Why would I?"

He put the book back down on the table. Etched out in graphite was a slender face with thick eyebrows and straight jaw-length hair. "Is that me?" I asked, genuinely impressed.

He slouched in his seat. "Yeah…"

I ruffled his hair. "Aw, you're such a girl."

"You said you wouldn't make fun of me," he pouted.

"It's great, Tony."

"Look, I drew mom too."

My mom was wrapping up the leftover pancakes in plastic.

"Can I talk to mom for a minute?" I asked Tony.

He got up from the table obediently.

"What sweetie?" she said, focusing on her task.

"I'm sorry."

She raised her eyebrows up at me. "What for?"

I gulped down the lump in my throat. "I'm sorry for hating you."

She stared at me, mouth gaping open. I just kept talking.

"I'm sorry Dad cheated on you, and I'm sorry for being mad at you for making us move, and I'm sorry for calling him...and I'm sorry for lying to you."

"What did you lie about?" she drug herself over to where I was sitting.

I lifted my butt off the seat and pulled the crumpled piece of paper out of my back pocket. Without saying another word, I shoved it at her.

She unfolded it and read it aloud. "This is from Denver...*Congratulations, due to your athletic achievement, you have been awarded..."* She stopped reading. "Andy... this is—"

I cut her off. "I got the letter way before we left." I bit my lip. "I don't wanna play soccer anymore. I hate soccer."

I waited for her to yell at me, or tell

me how much of a disappointment I was; or for her to tell me that it didn't matter what I wanted to do because I was doing it anyway, but she didn't say anything. She just examined the letter that was in her hands. Finally she spoke. "I'm glad you're home. I missed having you around the house."

"Mom..." I said still unsure.

"What honey?"

"Thanks."

Abigail lives with her family in Gladstone Oregon. She's studying English at Clackamas Community College and plans to transfer to Marylhurst. Abigail began writing her first book *Threads of Blue* her senior year of high school and plans to write many more. She is now twenty years old.

Support the author by reviewing this book on Amazon and Goodreads!

65129276R00084

Made in the USA
Charleston, SC
15 December 2016